Impetuous Women

Impetuous Women

SHIKHANDIN

PENGUIN
VIKING
An imprint of Penguin Random House

VIKING

USA | Canada | UK | Ireland | Australia
New Zealand | India | South Africa | China

Viking is part of the Penguin Random House group of companies
whose addresses can be found at global.penguinrandomhouse.com

Published by Penguin Random House India Pvt. Ltd
7th Floor, Infinity Tower C, DLF Cyber City,
Gurgaon 122 002, Haryana, India

Penguin
Random House
India

First published in Viking by Penguin Random House India 2021

Copyright © RK Biswas 2021

Shikhandin asserts the moral right to be identified as the author of this work.

All rights reserved

10 9 8 7 6 5 4 3 2 1

This is a work of fiction. Names, characters, places and incidents are either the
product of the author's imagination or are used fictitiously and any resemblance
to any actual person, living or dead, events or locales is entirely coincidental.

ISBN 9780670093199

Typeset in Minion Pro by Manipal Technologies Limited, Manipal
Printed at Thomson Press India Ltd, New Delhi

www.penguin.co.in

MIX
Paper
FSC FSC® C010615

For
Raagini Biswas

CONTENTS

Contents

TASTE

Sarita lifted a morsel of cheese from the plate and placed it gingerly on her tongue. She spat it out almost immediately.

'This one's gone bad. Fully!' she said wrinkling her nose. 'Why didn't you check, Dimple? *They* check us, no?'

Sarita spoke with the confidence of one who had undergone endless 'checks' herself. In reality, the stories she'd heard about the way Indians were treated at immigration checkpoints had been enough to convince her. The picture in her mind was indelible.

Dimple's mouth drooped. Her eyes turned moist with misery. She poured sweet milky tea into brand new cups. The cups looked refined and felt satiny smooth. But everybody she'd served tea to had remarked that you could buy the same cups and saucers (with matching dinner plates as well) in India just as easily. Dimple had also bought perfumes and lipsticks, but those too were available. Her friends and relatives had remained unimpressed with her shopping.

'What's the point of spending so much and going abroad for holidays?' Dimple had complained to Prakash. 'We may as well go to Kullu Manali in winter if we want to ski or throw snowballs.'

Prakash, however, had a different viewpoint, one which he reiterated with increasing force every passing year. According to Prakash's calculations, you actually paid less on a holiday abroad these days.

'You get better value,' he said. 'It's true, Dimple. What are basic amenities abroad are found only in five-star type hotels here. And, mind you, exorbitant five-star prices, not like there. But then, of course, only those who've gone abroad know,' he added with a smirk.

So, Dimple and Prakash continued to go overseas for holidays. Bangkok, Colombo, the Maldives, Hong Kong, Singapore, and then, Melbourne and Sydney, followed by cities in eastern Europe. They had just returned from Europe this time, after visiting the fashionable cities of Paris, Frankfurt, London and Venice. All duly stamped on their passports. Each time, they returned with things for themselves as well as their large circle of relatives and friends. In recent times (and Dimple had been noticing this with the silence of a helpless sufferer, even though Prakash remained, at least on the surface, oblivious), the presents she'd brought received little more than cursory glances and a polite 'thank you' or two, if at all. Her happiness over her cosmetics would have lost colour had Prakash not reassured her again and again of their true value.

'More or less,' he'd said. 'You get more or less the same brands and the same products. But,' and here he paused for effect, 'these are the latest. Factory-fresh. The ones here, and don't let the swanky malls fool you, Dimple, are at least six months old. I swear, it's still like that.'

Prakash's words were comforting and reassuring. Dimple had made wise purchases. Nobody realized what they were missing when they bought imported stuff that was at least a season old, thanks to India's import policies and the fact that the West could still get away with off-loading products their consumers had moved on from. Things that they paid exorbitant prices for at swanky malls in Chennai and Mumbai and Delhi. She shared Prakash's sagacious words with Sarita, just in case she planned a trip abroad, and Sarita nodded with the seriousness of one whose tickets and hotels were booked already.

And then Dimple had remembered the incident with the cheese.

She could have bought so many other things with the euros. But her pride had been at stake. The sudden silence, the looks cast their way, as if they were a bunch of savages. She was, after all, a representative of her country, wasn't she?

'I felt obliged, you know.'

'Oh?' Sarita studied Dimple's face while her own reflected a mixture of sympathy and irritation. 'Okay, I understand your sentiments,' she said after a pause. 'But we Indians are loud only, no? We are not cheater-cocks, are we? We are not showing people how cultured we are, and then robbing them of good money! We have our faults, no? Who's perfect? How many euros did you say?'

'Can't remember exactly,' Dimple shrugged. 'Thirty. Forty maybe.'

'Thirty–forty?' Sarita did a quick calculation on her fingers. '*Hai Ram*! You spent three to four thousand rupees on cheese? Just cheese?! What a waste!' She shook her head in disbelief. 'So much money for cheese? Including this half-blue half-white, smelling-so-bad fungus-wallah cheese! Honestly, Dimple, this is the height!' Sarita downed her tea in one gulp in protest.

Dimple stared at the offending item. All the joy from her Europe trip seemed to have congealed into this single stinky gob.

'Only this one's the worst,' she said at last. 'The others are quite nice. Sarita, taste *na*?' She pushed another floral-patterned plate with small wedges of different cheeses towards her.

Sarita looked at the plate. 'Very pretty designs, Dimple. Just like the one at Popatlal Jamal's. Only that one was a lovely purple shade. But I didn't buy. I have too many

4

purple things,' she said with a giggle. 'Anyway, which one of this lot is safe to eat?'

Dimple said nothing. Sarita pondered for almost half a minute before selecting a cream-coloured piece with holes in it. She took a tentative bite. 'No taste, ya. So bland.'

'It's nice with coriander chutney,' said Dimple, pushing a small porcelain bowl towards Sarita.

Sarita chewed a bit, considering the combination in her mouth before letting it slide down her throat. 'Better. But give me Amul any day!'

Dimple took a piece. 'Kraft is also good.'

Sarita, busy working her tongue on the bit that had got stuck to her upper palate, said, 'Kwaft is evwyware, ya.' She finally managed to get the cheese unstuck. Swallowing it, she continued, 'And that one also, what's it? That pizza-wallah cheese.'

'Mozzarella.'

'I know, babba! I know. It's everywhere these days.'

'You know why I went to the shop, Sarita?' said Dimple, peeling a piece off the plate. 'Because Kraft's so good I thought the ones in their shop would be even better. It's only for cheese, just imagine! A whole shop just for cheese! And so many types. My god, Sarita, they were giving samples for tasting. Free of cost!' She studied the cheese for a few seconds before placing it on her tongue.

'That's why your group members scrambled, and let their children loose!' said Sarita. 'It's this free mentality!

You can take Indians out of India but you can't take "free mentality" out of Indians. The kids vomited also, no? *Chhi chhi*! Big shame for us. What those foreigners must have thought!'

'Only one kid vomited. His father got so angry with the shopkeeper who was shouting in French. I don't know what all he said in French. All the people in the shop looked at us like we were . . . I can't tell you how bad I was feeling, you know.' Dimple shuddered at the memory. 'What could I do? At least you understand. But Prakash was so angry. "Oh, you and your pride," he said. Wasting good money!'

Sarita nodded in sympathy. 'Men don't understand, ya. They think more of money. But you know, Dimple, I agree with him also. See, this is plain cheating, isn't it? Look at this cheese, such nice packaging, and you said this one cost more, right?' Sarita thrust the cheese plate towards Dimple. 'Outside looking good. Inside all bad!'

'In India we are the exact opposite.'

'Yes!' said Sarita, and her smile expanded into a broad grin. 'And nothing beats Indian food! Whatever you say. Our taste is the best.'

Dimple grinned back, relieved the conversation had turned away from cheese. 'Correct! After three days we were hunting for Indian restaurants there! Anyway, Sarita let's leave this cheese-weez now. It's been so long. *Chal*, let's go eat some pani puri.'

'Ya, I know. Two weeks you spent there no, Dimple?'

'No, it was a twenty-one-day package. Europe with one-day shopping bonanza in Dubai. Free.'

'Free shopping in Dubai! Which travel agent?'

'No, ya. Only the trip; the stopover in Dubai was free. Some promo, you know.'

'Oh, yeah yeah. I know. Off-season package.'

Dimple was about to protest, but Sarita hurried on. 'I have to relieve Vipin. Let's hurry. There's a new shop near my house. Just opened. I heard their *chhole bhaturey* is to die for! And of course, the pani puris,' She grabbed her purse and stood up.

'One minute,' said Dimple and began clearing away the cups and plates.

She carefully dropped the cheeses into a Tupperware container, and closed the lid firmly, checking to see if it was airtight before placing the box in the refrigerator. Next, she placed the new cups and plates gently into a large plastic tub, which she hefted on to the kitchen platform. These she would wash herself when she returned; they were too precious to be entrusted to the maid. Dimple smiled to herself as she went about her chores watching Sarita shuffle her feet near the door. On the way to the pani puri shop she would get to hear the latest edition of Sarita's impending move to the US.

* * *

One look at Sarita's face and Vipin knew where she had been. He retreated into his laptop, even though his work for the day was over. The company he now worked for had recently started something called 'flexi-time', and Vipin took advantage of it more than he should have. Sarita didn't complain. He could stay home and babysit while she got her much-needed break from housework and her minimum-wage online job. The real reason why Vipin stayed at home was less pressure at work. The matter was worrying on one hand, but a godsend too, since they had a baby to take care of now. Vipin preferred to keep the worry part to himself. He'd rather change nappies and get baby food on his shirt than watch Sarita's blood pressure go up. Right now, since the baby was asleep and the dishes were done as well, his only escape route was the laptop. He needn't have bothered. Sarita ignored him and went straight to the kitchen. She banged the pots around for ten minutes before coming out to say that she wasn't in any mood to cook, so could he please go out and get something? ANYTHING EXCEPT PUNJABI, SOUTH INDIAN, MULTI-CUISINE, ITALIAN, CONTINENTAL! She was sick of the same menus, so could he for a change use his imagination and get something that looked and tasted more like food and less like oily-spicy-glop in foil boxes with wannabe-Westernized labels?

Vipin nodded and shuffled out of the room. Dinner was still a couple of hours away, but he'd rather be out driving in spite of the rush-hour traffic in Adyar than deal with Sarita's mood at home. He could use the opportunity to go to the Easwari Lending Library there and grab a couple of books, the latest Jeffrey Archer if he was lucky. Vipin took out his wallet from the cupboard and took a quick look at the infant sleeping on the bed. He was grateful her pot-banging hadn't woken him up. It had taken him more than an hour to get the little fella to sleep. He was also grateful Sarita hadn't mentioned pizza. That meant while any kind of pasta was out, pizza was in. Thank god for small mercies! Pizza didn't count as Italian, in an Italian–Italian sort of way. Pizza was universal food. Neither fast nor slow. Smartly American, but fulfilling in a nice Indianish-spicy sort of way; especially the Spice Garden vegetable pizza.

Vipin smacked his lips despite the tension trailing him like damp woodsmoke from their balcony. He wished she'd stop hanging out with Dimple, but Sarita seemed to be addicted. She had to have her Dimple fix every other week, especially after she returned from her twice-a-year holiday. Sarita always claimed afterwards that she'd put Dimple in her place, but Vipin knew better. He'd told her innumerable times that their time would come, sooner than she thought; he was only waiting for the right offer. That seemed to keep Sarita going, until she returned from Dimple's house, discouraged and unhappy, and the whole cycle would start all over again.

Vipin felt sorry for her. But more than her he felt sorry for himself. It would have been good for their son to have been born in the US, but the previous offer had fallen through even before Vipin had reached the crucial interview stage. Things had become so much tougher these days. Jobs were scarcer abroad than in India. Applying for an H1B visa was almost like asking for the moon! He should go to Hyderabad and pray to Visa-Balaji there. He had heard about that deity's fabulous boon-granting powers. It was worth a shot.

Vipin sighed as he eased the Maruti Swift (another bone of contention because Prakash and Dimple owned two cars, one of which was a Mercedes) into the only space left with barely a foot-and-a-half's gap between the parked vehicles. He wondered what today's story was going to be. Sarita's degree of unhappiness would depend on the intensity of her perceived humiliation.

* * *

Sarita moved listlessly around the house. She knew Vipin was trying, really trying. And she shouldn't be so hard on him. Besides, there was still a big demand for his line of work abroad, especially in the US. Who cared about Europe if you could go and live in California or Los Angeles? Once there, who cared whether you were a manager or not, or what your rank was. She'd heard that those things didn't matter out there, and that it was only in India that people asked about designations and so on. Of course, it would be tough, but in no time at all, they would be settled with a car and a house, just like the pictures her friends were posting on Facebook all the time. They were still young. Sarita had faith. She knew it was inevitable; she could almost taste the future. Even though the future seemed frustratingly fuzzy at this point in time. Even though so many Indians were returning despite having changed their citizenship! Sarita knew better. One had to live abroad for a few years at least. If you stayed long enough for a green card, and even better, a citizenship, and then returned, there was nothing like it. No holidays abroad could compare with having been an NRI. Sarita sighed and went and stood at the balcony.

She knew what Vipin was going to get. They could have ordered home delivery or 'takeout' as Dimple had begun to call it these days. But unbranded pizza was half the price, and tasted even better. At least they put more peppery pieces of paneer and mushrooms, though less cheese. But that could always be rectified by grating generous helpings of Amul cheese over the piping hot pizza. The thought of cheese took her back to the horrible thing she'd tasted earlier in the day. She almost gagged at the thought, and then a chuckle escaped her throat. Stupid Dimple! Sarita began to hum a song as she waited.

* * *

Dimple massaged her palms and feet with hand lotion. She smelt her arms, inhaling the faint floral scent pleasurably. Her pale-pink nightdress was short and she was glad she'd taken care to wax her legs the day before. Prakash had picked up the set for her from a little shop in Paris. She wanted him to see her looking pretty in it.

Afterwards, she gossiped softly about her day, and Prakash listened, drowsily at first, but suddenly he was awake again, and alert.

'Popatlal, my foot!' said Prakash. 'She's plain jealous. Next holiday we'll go to Canada. Tell her that.'

'Really?' said Dimple snuggling closer.

'Now we are doing business with the Canadians, remember? I told you!'

'Oh yes. *Chhi*! Forgot to tell Sarita,' Dimple hit her forehead.

'Good you didn't,' said Prakash. 'This dose should last for some time. Next time . . . Did you show her the videos I took?'

'Oh! Forgot that as well! All thanks to that cheese!'

'Uff, Dimple! That would've put her in her place.'

'I know. I know. She was so . . . Prakash, you should have heard her!' Dimple sat up impatiently. 'I feel for her and Vipin, you know. But she can be so irritating! Why is she like this only?'

Prakash drew her to him and squeezed her waist, '*Arrey*, who isn't? You tell me, is there anyone who isn't jealous of the other guy? Huh, tell me? Anyway, that's her problem. You don't go feeling sorry for her now, Dimple. Remember how people were to us? Remember?' And he gave her waist a little shake.

Dimple nodded. She hugged Prakash fiercely. A slight tremor rippled through her body. They rarely mentioned the early days.

'We have enough in the bank now, no Prakash?' she said with a quiver in her voice.

Prakash hoisted himself on his elbow and looked at her with serious eyes. 'Have faith in me and Sathya Sai Baba, Dimple. Have faith in Lord Venkateswara. The company's doing well. You wait and see,' Prakash stroked her hair. 'Don't worry. Just enjoy now, before our family grows.'

Dimple smiled at him, her eyes grew soft with love and faith, and the moment shimmered around them. But Prakash sat upright again, and slapped his knee, breaking the tender cocoon into which Dimple had let herself settle.

'So, we'll invite them over for dinner, *na*? I'll put on the videos. The look on their faces should make up for the euros we had to blow on your stupid cheese!'

It took Dimple a couple of seconds to understand what he was referring to. 'That's a good idea,' she said, more out of duty than anything else.

Prakash turned on his side and drifted off to sleep. Dimple stayed snuggled next to him, trying to find comfort in his warm body. But there was a sense of disquiet around her. There was this lingering feeling, an aftertaste in her mouth. Dimple wondered what the future would bring. A child, yes. And then? It was nice to dream. Prakash was also a lot more confident these days. But there were moments when Dimple wasn't so sure. How much of her destiny could she be in charge of? How much could their gods protect them? She wondered. They were after all just another couple among the billions sending prayers and donations to temples. Did Prakash understand? Perhaps they ought to buy more gold instead of squandering the money on foreign trips. And another house.

'Yes,' said Dimple softly to herself. 'Land and gold. Goddess Lakshmi's true gifts.'

Not perfumes, clothes and knick-knacks from abroad. Who cared about Western food anyway? They would always return to the comfort of dal–roti–*sabzi*. And hot *gulab jamuns*. The thought of the syrupy sweets warmed her. She would broach the subject tomorrow, she told herself, as she slid a hand under Prakash's elbow and threaded her fingers into the wiry hair on his chest.

'Perhaps a farmhouse,' she mused drowsily. Farmhouses were the trend. With organic vegetables growing in your own garden. For better health, for better taste. And to show the world you'd truly arrived.

JUST DESSERTS

Liese was a precise kind of woman. She liked to stick to a schedule; she liked law and order; she followed precise recipes. She blinked at the recipe card when she made her irresistible melt-in-the-mouth chocolate mousse. She knew the recipe by heart, but she blinked three times for luck each and every time she made her Indian special—steeped in sugar—chocolate mousse.

Liese never used the electric beater. She always whipped the cream by hand for the same number of strokes that had produced her first fluffy, light-as-air mousse. She made it a point to beat the egg whites until they reached that Santa's cap-point of stiffness. She did everything with precision because her chocolate mousse was a dessert that demanded it. Liese knew that. She knew that she was born to create such desserts. Perfect in their perfection; predictably perfect in their texture and flavour. Of all the dishes that Liese cooked with élan, her desserts were the best. Of all the desserts that Liese created with panache, her chocolate mousse was her pièce de résistance. Liese attributed her culinary skills to her love for precision.

The only imprecise thing that Liese had ever done in her life was to marry Dinesh. Her German family had been surprised by her choice. Dinesh did not fit in with their notion of what they supposed was Liese's idea of a perfect husband. He was not Indian royalty. He was not a brilliant scholarship-holder with poetry flowing in his veins. He was not an artist. He was not a savvy accountant. He was neither tall nor short, fat or thin. Altogether he fell somewhere in between.

Liese's friends in Hamburg and her aunts from Frankfurt were confident she would come out of her infatuation. Her parents in Berlin believed that the blurred edges of their relationship would finally dissipate and she would see the light of day. Her ex-boyfriend in Nuremberg telephoned her, asking her to stop the nonsense. Dinesh was after all a man whose antecedents were utterly obscure. Her ex also assured her he was not trying to get back into her life, but merely trying to make her see sense for old time's sake. Liese was certain she would prove all the naysayers wrong. She married Dinesh and moved to Mandoli, Shahdara, in northeast Delhi, with all her recipe books.

Life in Mandoli turned out to be very different from what she had imagined it to be. She would have chosen something else, another place at least, but Dinesh had already happened in her life and Mandoli was where his family business flourished. So that would have to be that, in spite of Liese's misgivings.

Mandoli simply couldn't seem to move on precisely oiled wheels. It chugged and sputtered, belched and smoked, and stopped in the middle of important things. There were air-conditioned malls and departmental stores where she could pick up zucchini and leek, taste teeny wedges of cheese before making her selection. There was wine as well, from all around the world, though priced much higher than what they were worth. But the city left her muddled with its unruly mix of colours and textures. Its strong aromas nearly brought about fainting spells. But Liese was made of sterner stuff. She taught herself to live without absolute precision, with slightly stale bratwurst and Christmas stollen that was just that teeny bit off. She learnt to pin her hopes on Dinesh's absolute faith in his country. She loved him. She believed him. She managed to pull through, sometimes almost by the skin of her teeth.

Over the years, she learnt to tolerate pollution and tardiness, watch out for lazy watchmen who let in suspicious-looking characters but never failed to harass the delivery boys. She learnt to keep an eagle eye out for thieving maids who would otherwise pick her dresser clean.

She learnt to dodge cowpats in the by lanes and alleyways of Delhi's old parts that beckoned her with their mysteries. She taught herself to look beyond the wall-squirting men and open-drain-squatting naked children. With time, Liese became Indian enough to feel a twinge of nerves at India's *modern* developments. Meanwhile, there were all those uniquely Indian luxuries that she learnt to enjoy, like being driven around everywhere in a chauffeured car and having an entourage of people who were more than willing to run errands for her.

Liese spent her days learning yoga and batik-printing. She hobnobbed with poets, artists, businessmen and politicians. Dinesh was a rising entrepreneur. Liese's life, after the initial hiccups were over, became good and steady, which was how she wanted it to be. Little things like the voltage fluctuations in summer, when her oven turned cranky and belched out cracked cakes with soggy insides and the toaster expelled either underdone toasts or bread slices burnt to a crisp, bothered her far less than they used to before. Meanwhile, her chocolate mousse became a legend. And it was precisely her skill with this dessert that brought Poornima into her life.

Doe-eyed, black-haired, lithe and sexy Poornima spoke huskily and moved about enveloped in an aura of musk. Who could resist her? Had Liese been born and raised in India, she would have not only resisted Poornima, but would have been able to keep her out completely, without messing up her rebonded hair, and saved herself much bother afterwards. But Liese didn't believe that a bimbo like Poornima could do much harm. Besides, she was already married to Shekhar, who was unapologetically rich and madly in love with Poornima. So, what was the problem? None, initially, when the two couples met and became fast friends over rich after-dinner helpings of Liese's chocolate mousse.

Within a short span of time, Poornima and Liese became close enough to go on shopping trips. They started going to art exhibitions together. They practised henna tattoos on each other and even wished each other on their birthdays with flowers and cake. Liese got used to Poornima's presence in her house during most mornings and sometimes in the afternoons when Liese worked on her dessert recipes. Dinesh got used to Poornima's long phone calls, precisely at nine at night when he most wanted to have sex with Liese. After some time, he started enjoying her calls and made Liese put her on speakerphone, while he laughed into her breasts, and shook the bed violently with his thrusts and shaking shoulders.

Liese didn't guess a thing. She remained blissfully unaware for a very long time. The nickel didn't drop even when she called Poornima in the mornings, sharp at 11 a.m., and heard muffled gibberish in the background. But things like this do not stay undercover for long. And, the day arrived when Liese became wise. Her new-found wisdom, instead of making her happier and calmer, like a person who has accepted her karma, actually turned her into a bubbling cauldron of rage; the kind in which thick custard bubbles up in little stinging spits, and you have to keep the heat really low to prevent the goop from burning.

Liese's mind raged and howled, even though she expressed nothing outwardly. She kept the hatred bottled and sealed inside her for a very long time. So long that she once thought that perhaps she had learnt to live with it, like she had with the rest of the things in India. But the anger spat up its bile every now and then, and with increasing frequency as the days went by. That was alarming. Liese realized she would go mad if she let things be just as they were. She had to do something about it.

More than invention, necessity is the mother of creativity. Once Liese had mentally accepted that she had to do something, her brain started to sort out and stack all kinds of ideas for revenge. Finally, Liese chose one, which she fervently hoped would bring finality into her life with the precision of a knife's edge. Of course, there was bound to be temporary havoc initially, but in the long run she would be able to return to a steady, uncomplicated existence, except for a few major changes, once her plan materialized. She felt at peace after her decision, and a cool breeze seemed to blow on her skin. Liese strategized as she cooked; she plotted as she gossiped; she schemed as Dinesh giggled into her breasts precisely at 9 p.m. every night.

The blueprint blossomed. A structure began to take shape and the finer details started pouring in. Her daily routine went on. Nothing changed on the surface. Everything was as cool as the milky skin over freshly made kheer, and you would never know how hot it was inside until you dipped your finger. But Poornima loved Liese's chocolate mousse even more. Dinesh liked it too, though not as much as the many Indian desserts that Liese had so painstakingly learnt to perfect over the years. So Liese got to work, but first she did some detailed research.

Finding the right ingredients was not as difficult as Liese had initially thought; perhaps it was because she had taught herself to lob and catch life pretty deftly in India by then. Besides, Shrivastav, her chauffeur, a quiet and dependable hill fellow was fiercely loyal. Liese knew no one would know where she had been going in the mornings, when she ought to have been chatting with Poornima on the phone at home. Sometimes Liese called her from her cell phone to make sure Poornima and Dinesh (yes, him too!) did not get suspicious. Delhi's labyrinths had many strange shops that kept all kinds of ingredients, colourless and odourless, liquids and powders, which were easy to mix and match in precise quantities. Shrivastav would do the legwork for her without any questions, while Liese sat in the air-conditioned comfort of her car, incognito behind her sunglasses. Liese had become quite fond of the young man. He was such a sincere dear, slogging away for his wife and family to enjoy the money he posted to them every month. Poornima's driver in contrast was a cheeky fellow who was forever chewing paan. But Poornima being the low-class slut that she was couldn't be expected to survive without her dose of daily gossip, even if it meant being familiar with a servant.

Friday night arrived. A marmalade-coloured moon shed soft romantic light on the porch. A pleasant September night, with a rich velvety purple sky, and the scent of late-blooming jasmine everywhere. The perfect time. Liese's plan was to have dinner, all four of them together, at her farmhouse. She truly surpassed herself that day. The success of her dinner, from start to finish, depended on her and her alone.

The dinner would begin with a light consommé. The next dish on the menu would be baked escargots and then they would move on to the main dish of pepper roast and stir-fried greens on the side. Bottles of Chablis and Châteauneuf-du-Pape would be on the bar counter, cool and inviting. But Liese also remembered to keep cans of soda water for Dinesh who could never comprehend the subtlety of good wine and had to get his kicks from Johnnie Walker Black Label and Chivas Regal, in spite of living with Liese for all these years. Why couldn't he at least cultivate a taste for Macallan or even Glenfiddich? Liese sighed and smoothened her newly highlighted hair.

The excitement of making the extra-special mousse had tired her out, so she decided to take a siesta in the afternoon. Poornima, who had popped in to see if Liese needed any help, obligingly massaged her head and neck with fragrant oil. Liese fell asleep, feeling soothed and contented, and so much at peace.

The dinner was a success. Everybody was charming, and the food was perfect. Everything was happening the way Liese had envisaged it. The conversation was light and witty. The end-of-summer air was fragrant and cool. Liese looked charming in a sapphire silk suit. 'It goes so well with your grey eyes,' Dinesh said kissing her cheek. And then it was time for dessert.

'Dessert time!' Poornima trilled, as if the whole thing was her own handiwork. 'You sit and sip your Bristol Cream Sherry, dahling!' she said to Liese, 'You still look a wee bit tired. Let me serve today.'

There was nothing that Poornima could do to Liese's chocolate mousse even if she was hell-bent on adding her individual touch to it. It would start to melt if you left it out too long, and Poornima wouldn't do anything so obvious. So, Liese relaxed with her glass. From the corner of her eyes, she could see Poornima bustling around her pantry with practised ease. The 'practised ease' bit irritated Liese, but she sipped the feeling away with sherry.

The dessert arrived in individual crystal bowls. Shekhar, who had recently been diagnosed with diabetes, declined, apologizing profusely to Liese. He thanked her equally profusely for the dish of fresh fruits she put had put out for him. Poornima beamed at everyone, as if it was she who had made the mousse. She and Dinesh dug into their bowls, and a watchful silence descended.

'Wasn't that delicious?' said Dinesh to nobody in particular.

'Why, thank you!' exclaimed Poornima, before Liese could put in a word. She stood up like she had something important to say. Liese gaped. Poornima hadn't toppled over. As for Dinesh, instead of slumping into his chair and becoming stiff, he beamed at everyone, looking as fit as a fiddle.

'And now for the surprise, everybody,' Poornima sang, almost gleefully.

'What surprise?' said Liese, beginning to feel ill.

'Well,' said Poornima, with a sexy sway of her hips. 'You see, it's my chocolate mousse that you all ate today! I've been watching you Liese . . . Oh, don't look so shocked, dahling, I only watch you in the kitchen . . .'

Dinesh laughed out loud at the joke, as if he was the only one who was privy to it. And Shekhar's face went a shade pale. Liese only gripped the arm of her chair. Poornima carried on with her hip swaying, until Liese began to turn a speckled shade of spinach green.

'Everybody simply loooooves your chocolate mousse, Liese, dear girl! So, I thought to myself, "Poornima, why don't you try it out and see?" So, I did, and I simply switched the two in the afternoon. Simple. Did you like it, Dinesh?'

Liese could feel a shiver running down her spine, but she steadied herself, taking care to keep her voice neutral. 'That's wonderful, dear. But what did you do with the one I had made?'

'Oh, that,' said Poornima airily. 'I gave that to your Shrivastav.'

'But Shrivastav is a vegetarian! He doesn't even eat eggs!' Liese could feel her hysteria rising in a solid mass as her brain screamed, 'Not Shrivastav! No, god! No. No!' The sherry turned rancid in her throat.

'My dear, I told him so. But he said that if it was made by Liese Memsaab, he would not mind eating a bit of egg,' Poornima giggled. 'Seemed to me he'll gladly eat even poison from your hands, dahling!'

THRESHOLD

Women like her are unlovable creatures. Yet, it is love they hunger for. From you, your husband, your child, your home . . . If they could, they'd suck it clean from your life, like the sweet cold juice of popsicles.

Of course, you'd hated her. On sight.

Her story was no different from the stale old tales you'd heard before from the mouths of similar women. You barely believed her when she told you she'd been married off at a young age, and later, after three stillborn children, had been unceremoniously dumped by her husband. Another man had taken her in after that. She'd borne him a son and a daughter. They'd been happy, until they were swept up one day without warning into the tidal wave of minorities trying to flee their country. Overnight, they'd become hated aliens in their own backyards. Your lips had curled involuntarily. Hundreds of stories, exactly like hers, were crawling all over Kolkata, looking for kind-hearted fools.

No other Indian metropolis had seen such a continuous influx of illegal immigrants, year after year, slithering in to seek asylum. Despised and distrusted, they—the eyesores of your society—worked in the homes of decent people, providing relief for working women like you. Of course, that didn't mean you had to trust them. Heaven knew what they'd done and where they'd been. Domestic work was not the only trade these women practised. You'd heard horror stories about them worming their way in, taking over the whole house, and at times the husbands as well. But someone had to be there when you were away. One couldn't always depend on part-time maids supervised by your in-laws. Not that they'd mind; maids weren't the only ones who set out to take control of your life. In this country, daughters-in-law always got the stick, especially the working ones.

There were days when, drained of life, you'd collapse on your bed, wondering how your position was any better than that of a refugee. Despite your law-given marital domain, you felt like an outsider, so often literally begging to be let into your husband's family, and wondering at the same time if it was worth the trouble at all.

The first thing she'd said, when you were negotiating her terms and salary, was, 'If you give me love, *boudi*, I'll lay my life down for you.'

You made it a point to keep your steel cupboard locked. Then again, everything in the house couldn't be locked up, could it? A woman like that and the least she'd steal were your cosmetics and food. Your husband complained about the cupboard at first, but buckled under your hard stare. You took your son to school yourself, and requested your parents-in-law (who lived nearby, thanks to your husband's assiduous planning) to bring him back every day. You knew you were playing into their hands by taking favours. It was hard but you did it, because no matter how nasty your in-laws were to you, you knew you could trust them completely when it came to their own grandchild.

It didn't take the woman long to make herself comfortable in your house. She ate food that was not hers to eat. She slept on your bed when you weren't there. The imprint of her head on your pillow, and the scent of the hair oil she used, yours which she helped herself to, gave her away. When you confronted her, she grinned and said she needed a proper bed. Madam wasn't satisfied with her cotton mattress on the floor.

She liked to talk in the evenings, whenever you returned early from work, about her life, and her great escape. She said she used to hide among the water hyacinths in her village pond. Day after day, she and a few others, women of varying age groups, would creep out of their homes before sunrise and sink without a splash in the pond. With their faces hidden among the lush growth, they'd stay submerged until dark, the sun beating down on their concealed but unprotected heads, while the water grew chillier by the hour. They gritted their teeth when they felt cold, that was all. They didn't even stir when the baby carp nibbled at their feet and legs. They lived in silence and darkness, taking care to walk on the vegetation bordering the pond, so no one could spot their footprints on the moist clay path. They ate whatever they could lay their hands on, quickly and furtively, not daring to suck and chew on the odd fish bone lest they be heard. They took care to wipe out all signs of their existence on dry land every day, before dawn tore up night's mantle of invisibility.

She'd sit on the floor, drinking tea from a steel cup. She had a habit of puckering up her mouth, as if squeezing out a punctuation mark from her lips when she paused. You watched her staring at a point beyond you, rocking on her haunches to the beat of her memories.

There were soldiers everywhere, she said; men and women disappearing every day. Sometimes a woman came back, either torn up too badly or just plain dead, which was better anyway, and she nodded into her cup. Better to be dead than torn up like that. Besides, who would claim or name the child born? We helped them die, she said, and you shivered, but she held your eyes. There were herbs and things that eased more than pain.

Three months, she said, three months we hid among the water hyacinths. The skin of my hands and feet was so corrugated from the constant wetness, boudi, you could wring out water from them to drink. Then the night came when we got a chance, and escaped. My husband—and she made a face, her lips almost spitting out the word—went that way with our son; she pointed towards the north. My daughter and I came here . . . I've found a nice home for my daughter, an old couple. Better to keep her with an old couple. That way, even if the man's wicked, he won't be up to much harm. She laughed in a vulgar, knowing way.

What happened to your husband? You asked coldly, hating her for making you curious.

Her face turned stony. I don't know. I never heard from him for a long time. Now I hear that he's alive . . . trying to come here. But there are more jobs for women in Kolkata. There are always more jobs for women . . . So men get used to sitting at home and eating. Maybe that's why he wants me now. What was he doing all this time? We crossed over to India, at different points in the border, but everybody knew I was heading for Kolkata. Why now? Why not then? She got up to pop a bone in her lower spine, arch her back and yawn. But he's my man, can't let him go just like that, can I? Someday, soon, my daughter will need a husband. The boy's family will want to know who the father is. I can't call myself a widow. That would bring god's wrath on my poor daughter. See, she said showing off the red and white bangles on her wrists, I still wear my *shankha* and *pola*.

She also wore a big red dot on her forehead, but nothing in the parting of her hair. Why don't you wear vermilion? You asked, unable to help yourself.

She grinned like a shark. My hair's sensitive; you know how careful I have to be with the hair oil.

The neighbours complained that they'd seen her combing her hair on the balcony with long slow strokes and speaking loudly with someone on the street below. They said she went out as soon as you left for work. You knew you were buying far too much food, detergent and toiletries. A couple of your good cotton saris had disappeared.

Once she placed her elbows on your husband's chair, leaning over him as he sat at the table eating dinner. He sprang up, startled, even frightened. But she remained unfazed, a curious expression lighting up her face, as if she was the soldier, and he, a hapless woman. Had crossing the border made her that way? What had she lost? What had she become? You saw the fierceness of her lust for life and grew afraid. You wondered if you would ever be able to get rid of her. It wouldn't be easy. Such women, once they entered your home, stuck on like burrs. Any move to throw them out usually ended up in ugly scenes, with the neighbours being privy. Sometimes even the jobless young men, who played cards and carom on sidewalks, and acted as if they owned the locality, entered homes to harangue and humiliate the family. There'd been cases of police harassment as well. Women like her knew how to use men.

Then suddenly, she disappeared for the whole day, returning way past midnight. Your husband, with sleep-tousled hair and pyjamas but without the top, opened the door and froze. She burst into your house, wild-eyed and dishevelled. You confronted her angrily, but she ignored you.

Didn't you hear me? You screamed, not caring about the neighbours. Who do you think you are? Is this your father's hotel, going and coming as you please?

She spun around to face you. Witch! She said. Witch has taken my man. May her skin rot! Rot with leprosy. Her bones crumble! She collapsed into an incoherent heap, clutching the edges of your nightdress, moaning, boudi, o boudi.

Not knowing what else to do, you left her a plate of rice and dal, and went to bed. She seemed normal the next morning, though somewhat surly. She made tea, and went about her chores. But when you returned home, you found the front door unlocked. She was nowhere to be seen. Your first concern was whether she'd taken anything. You asked around the apartment complex. The watchman said he'd seen her. So had the sweeper, and the other maids. That was all; nobody had any specific information. They all wanted to know if there was anything missing.

You decided to do a thorough search of your home, though you weren't sure of what you were going to look for. The gaps and spaces left behind by missing items? Clues? Secrets? Whatever it was, you decided you'd know it when you saw it.

You discovered things that you'd stashed away and forgotten all about. Things that took you back to a time in your life that you had tucked away into a far corner of your heart for safekeeping. Your head billowing with memories, you continued your search until you reached the small room at one end of your apartment. The room was not quite a servant's room, more like an extra bedroom or study, but without an attached bathroom. There was a smell in it that made you feel unclean, like an intruder. You'd rarely entered the room when she was around. You checked the mattress, more for stains than for anything else. What annoyed you most was she had left without washing her sheets. You would have to pay the part-time maid, the one who came to sweep and mop every morning, extra money to wash it. There was nothing underneath the mattress, an obvious place for maids to stash things. There were two cupboards, a bookcase and a writing desk fitted together and built into one of the walls. You'd allowed her to keep her belongings in one of the cupboards. The other housed sundry items like lampshades, table linen, crockery and decorative knick-knacks—whims that you'd collected, but rarely found any use for. None of them had much resale value. Maids wouldn't bother to steal them, except out of sheer viciousness. Everything was intact. Only the cupboard where she kept her belongings was bare, save for a few loose sheets of newspaper. You gingerly picked up the ends of the papers and shook them. An envelope fell out and slid across the floor.

It contained a small packet of musty-smelling vermilion and a postcard-sized black-and-white photograph of a small girl in a frock with a doll in her arms. The doll was dressed up like a Hindu bride. A little boy sat across from her, smiling self-consciously. In his hands he held another doll, dressed up in a skullcap, shirt and lungi. His doll had a beard scratched on its cheeks with a black pen or eye-pencil. The children were sitting atop a table, surrounded by happy-faced men and women. Curious, you peered for details. Not all the men and women were Hindus; it was obvious from the way they were dressed. The little girl, fair and sharp-featured, was clearly her.

What had compelled her to carry the photograph of a make-believe wedding, a doll's wedding, with her across the border? What woman would choose a photograph over everything else? The grown-ups in the picture were indulging two children. It was just fun and games, and they had got into the spirit of it. That much was clear. Then, with a start you understood what it was that fuelled the volcano in her heart. Her husband was not the one she was after, not in the true sense. It was something far more elusive. It was something that perhaps no longer existed in your own life.

Memories fluttered agitatedly in your head. Your past life began to zigzag before you like a movie run amok. You sat as if hypnotized in that unhealthy hour before night, when smoky darkness swarms in, filling up the corners of rooms with dread. A sharp chill entered your bones, when a thought without precedence arose and slapped against the piers of your mind: *what could you possibly take if you had to leave this life suddenly?* And the words carried in them the cruel cry of urchins killing a dog.

You sat there without light, ignoring the timid hum of your empty house, and tried to be a reasonable, rational being. A stupid maid's departure shouldn't drive you insane. Nevertheless, the prospect of continuous housework frightened you; not so much for the work but for the dread of becoming tied down, of having to give up your freedom, your salary, and your very identity. And there was that noiseless tugging at your innards as well, from which another face, thin and intense, with the pencil shadow of a moustache, that face from your past, bobbed up, as nebulous as a pond blossom in the morning mist.

The doorbell brought you back with a jolt. It was the newspaperman; he had come to collect his dues. Afterwards, you turned on the lights in every single room. An unnameable emotion turned your limbs doughy and clumsy. You made yourself a cup of tea with effort, and sat down with it to watch a sitcom on TV you'd never cared for before. After some time, you found yourself returning to the photograph. Turning it over in your hand, you idly wondered how she'd managed to keep it dry among the water hyacinths, day after day. Or had she retrieved it from its hiding place on the day of her flight?

Suddenly, the sky seemed to split apart with the light of clarity. This woman, who had loved so hungrily and fought with so many forces, had seen through your heart's lean diet. Every hair on your back, standing stiff and alert, told you that she had gauged the distance between you and your husband, and patrolled the separate silent terrains that you both now occupied. She had discovered the barren spaces in your life, which should have remained crowded with loving things. But you had also discovered something with your woman's instinct. You knew that she would return to reclaim her treasure. And that you would give it back to her. The matter would end there. You wouldn't ask her to resume work, even if it meant giving your son up to your in-laws.

You rose to rinse your cup, muttering under your breath, and the house obediently absorbed your words. For wasn't this your territory, no matter how sterile?

Respectability was the carapace beneath whose protection you'd spent your entire life. Your identity had never suffered any puncture from political and religious disharmony. Your roots went much deeper than that of water hyacinths. Your feet had never had any need to shy away from bare wet clay, ever. So, all that you had to do now was to shut that door on her. Her and her knowing eyes. Her and her endlessly seeking heart. You had to shut that door so hard that nobody, and certainly not she, could get in. Some borders should never be breached. Never. Never. You told yourself, as you stood there, surveying your domain with certainty, even as your eyes brimmed over with the acid rain of defeat.

MIZ TIGA DOES NOT PLAY HOLI

Miz Tiga watched the girls from the window of her tiny parlour. They were shouting and giggling, pushing and jostling, with an abandon that only a bunch of giddy schoolgirls could possess. Miz Tiga adjusted the steel-rimmed spectacles on her nose. She gave the girls one last stern look before returning to the kitchenette behind her parlour.

The girls were excited because the next three days were school holidays. None of them would be going home for the weekend though. They would rather stay back for this particular long weekend, because of the Holi festival.

Miz Tiga did not like Holi. She did not like giggly schoolgirls either. But the combination of giggly schoolgirls and Holi (which was the messiest festival, worse than Diwali, in her opinion!) gave Miz Tiga a headache.

The other teachers at school knew she did not play Holi, so they left her in peace, apart from sending over a plate or two of sweetmeats. The girls knew Miz Tiga did not approve of scatterbrained girls in full Holi regalia (colour-sodden clothes and faces 'monkeyed' with gulal!) so they usually stayed away from her portion of the teachers' quarters.

The teachers' quarters were made up of two rows of red-tiled single- and double-bedroomed cottages at one end of the vast school compound. Each cottage had its own small patch of garden, separated from one another and the school compound as well by hibiscus hedges trimmed low. These dwarf borders gave one a clear view of the wide gravelled path that ran between the two rows of cottages, and also of any person who happened to be on that path, just as the cluster of girls was, on that bright and clear, late spring evening.

Dusk was still a long way off. And the birds were still busy going about their business; the evening chatter of homing birds would not commence for another hour or so. The school was in the lull period between the end of classes and the gong for dinner, when the girls were free to loiter around the grounds. Miz Tiga savoured this hour when she could make herself a cup of sweet milky tea in her kitchenette and drink it in the quiet comfort of her double-bed-sized front porch. She did not want chattering girls nearby when she drank her tea slowly, sip by savoured sip, as she rocked gently in her cane rocking chair. But habit is habit after all. And a bunch of giddy girls was not going to keep Miz Tiga away from her cup of tea.

Miz Tiga placed her cup on the cane side table. It was actually more of a coffee mug than a teacup, made from heavy lily china, criss-crossed with age. It had a rotund figure line-drawn in black with the legend 'MRS' on it. There was another just like it, except for the legend that said 'MR', stashed away in the cupboard behind her dining table in one corner of her parlour. She had bought the pair years ago, when she was a young wife, when Mr Tiga shared her quiet evening tea.

Now she sipped her tea, looking covertly through her glasses. The girls were still there, gathered in front of Mrs Bose's gate. Mrs Bose, thin as a reed and ready to burst into fits of giggles just like her charges, was obviously their favourite teacher. Her popularity would always increase before Holi, because she was in charge of getting the girls organized for the festival. The girls were probably trying to find out how much gulal and how many packets of colour for the coloured water each of them would be allotted. They would not be told, no matter how much they begged and cajoled Mrs Bose. But undeterred, they would debate about the ration of colours both wet and dry, and try to include Mrs Bose in their debate, in the childish hope that she would let some vital information slip. Mrs Bose knew the game and she played along, much to Miz Tiga's disgust. A stern 'come back tomorrow, girls!' would have cut down this unseemly cacophony immediately. But Mrs Bose seemed to enjoy the whole business.

Miz Tiga listened with half an ear to the girls' chatter, punctuated by Mrs Bose's cackling laugh. She laughs like a hyena, thought Miz Tiga irritably. This was not really true, but 'laughing like a hyena' was Miz Tiga's favourite expression, especially when she reprimanded the girls about their uncontrollable sense of humour. She had other expressions in her arsenal, which she used indiscriminately on the girls; but when she flung it at an unwary teacher, usually the younger and more inexperienced ones, she did condescend to exercise a pinch of tact.

Very few teachers crossed words with her, as she was one of the oldest teachers in the school. Miz Tiga had been teaching Hindi and moral science for more than thirty years. Nobody remembered Miz Tiga as a young woman, though thirty years ago she certainly had been young, and contentedly married to Mr Tiga. She did not live in her cottage on the school grounds then. She came to school in a Morris Minor car, driven by Mr Tiga, who regularly dropped his wife at her school on his way to office.

'But Miz Tiga doesn't play Holi!'

The thin birdlike voice, probably Navjit's, who could never stop herself from saying the wrong thing at the right place and the right thing at the wrong time, rose above the chatter, and an awkward silence descended immediately.

The girls and Mrs Bose knew Miz Tiga was sitting on her porch and drinking her tea, as usual.

Miz Tiga stiffened. Her glasses caught the setting sun's rays and glowed red.

'Now girls! Everybody doesn't have to get wet and covered from head to toe in gulal in order to enjoy Holi. Some of us like to watch . . .'

'But miss, she wouldn't like us to go to her. I mean like we come to you and the other teachers for sweets an' all. I mean . . .' This was said in a low voice.

'Probably Dipti, the most outspoken of the lot,' thought Miz Tiga grimly. She had stopped rocking and was listening keenly.

'Now, now girls!' said Mrs Bose again. This time she tried to make her voice a bit sterner. 'You must respect your teachers and other seniors and do your part. Doesn't Miz Tiga distribute cakes during Christmas? You must wish her "Happy Holi". Okay? Now run along. You don't want to be late for dinner. You have to wash up first, you know!'

With that she shooed the girls away and walked quickly inside, but not before Dipti had piped up with, 'But, miss, we are never here during Christmas!'

The girls dispersed. Their disgruntled chatter wafted towards Miz Tiga in muffled tones. She did not have to hear the exact words to know what they were grumbling about. Everybody in the school knew that not only did Miz Tiga not play Holi, she disapproved of any activity that involved mess and grime and shouting and screaming. She did not like hysterical girls. She had no patience with teachers who could not instil discipline in the students. She was especially strict with Christian girls, who habitually incurred her wrath for sundry offences that ranged from long nails and stray curls to not knowing the Bible as well as they ought. Miz Tiga knew she was not popular with the girls. She also knew that they cracked many jokes and mimicked her behind her back.

Miz Tiga got up from her comfortable position and walked down to the wooden gate that separated her cottage from the path.

'Girls!' she barked. 'Come here!'

The girls froze. They slowly retraced their steps until they were standing between her cottage and that of Mrs Bose.

'Yes, miss?' They said in a united whisper, huddling like frightened chicks.

'Tomorrow, in the evening, after you are done playing and have cleaned yourselves, you may come to wish me "Happy Holi". Okay?'

'Yes, miss!' they said in unison again and started to flee towards the main school building; all the girls, except one.

This was none other than Navjit, the owner of the thin birdlike voice. The rest of her matched her voice, for she was a thin small child with two long thin braids, and grazed elbows and knobby knees.

'Why, miss?' she asked, not rudely, though the choice of words was wrong, while a gasp of shock shuddered through the rest of the girls.

'According to the traditional rules of Holi, you play with your friends, but pay respect to elders by putting a bit of gulal on their feet!' she said. 'And elders give sweets,' she added, squeezing back a smile that had timidly started out at the corner of her thin lips.

Navjit looked at her wide-eyed. 'Yes, miss,' she replied with saucer eyes.

The rest of the girls said nothing. They could barely suppress their giggles. They quickly walked back the way they had come, their giggles growing bolder as the distance between them and Miz Tiga increased.

'And elders give sweets,' mimicked Sudha, instantly provoking peals of laughter from the rest.

'My god, Miz Tiga's sweets!' said Dipti. She turned to her companions. 'Remember what she gave us last year?'

'Yeah! Stone-hard sesame laddus,' said Sudha.

'And they were old too,' said Elizabeth, wrinkling her nose at the memory.

'She brought them out from a rusty ol' Nespray tin! Yuck!' said Dipti.

'I think we should go,' said Navjit seriously.

'Yes, *chumchy*, you go!'

'As if toadying to ol' Tiga's going be of any use!'

Navjit took the jibes in her stride. Something in Miz Tiga's manner had struck a chord in her heart. But she knew confiding in her friends would make them taunt her more. Meanwhile, Miz Tiga hurried inside. She would be up early tomorrow. The girls had no idea how much one had to prepare if one wanted to celebrate Holi properly. They did not know that Holi was not just about getting dirty and gorging on sweets. But how could they? Times have changed, she told herself as she rolled out the two chapattis she made for her dinner every day. Miz Tiga looked up, cocked her head and almost smiled. She could almost hear Mr Tiga stirring the big pot of milk on the stove in preparation for the bhang-laced sherbet for Holi.

Mr Tiga did not drink or smoke. Miz Tiga would never have agreed to the match if he did. Most of his friends were not averse to drinking. But Mr Tiga restricted his drinking to that sip of communion wine at Sunday church, and the solitary glass of brandy before Christmas dinner. But bhang was something he drank every Holi.

Miz Tiga did not mind. It had never occurred to her not to participate in this Hindu festival. Her parents had always joined in the mirth and merriment of Holi, just as their Hindu friends had never forgotten to call on them during Christmas. And bhang was such an integral part of Holi!

'Miz Tiga,' she heard him say as she worked in her kitchenette. 'Miz Tiga, make sure the pistachios are well-ground for my special bhang.'

Mr Tiga always called her Miz Tiga, never Susan Mary. And she always called him Mr Tiga, never by his first name, which was Thomas.

They would both be up and awake by dawn on the day of Holi. Mr Tiga would softly hum to himself as he made coffee for both of them. Miz Tiga would bustle around the kitchen as she made her preparations for the morning. There would be a mound of laddus and *mawa* barfis and some savoury snacks to be made. And of course the bhang sherbet had to be kept ready and chilled in a large earthen pitcher that was brought out from the storeroom before Holi every year.

She would also prepare lunch beforehand. That part was easy though. After consuming so many sweetmeats, there would be little room for anything more than a bit of fried vegetables and khichri. But she would not skimp on the quantity, because on the day of Holi, you never knew how many people would be having lunch at your place. And Mr Tiga had a large circle of friends, not necessarily Ranchi Christians like themselves, for the town where Mr Tiga lived was a very cosmopolitan town. And most of their friends worked at the same factory as Mr Tiga.

Miz Tiga would watch Mr Tiga as he ambled out of the house in his white pyjama and matching white kurta. He would look like a child with his favourite toy, never mind the silver strands sneaking up to catch the sun on his head. He would fill the brass bucket with water and test the brass water gun that he would use to spray coloured water on his friends.

The girls in the school used flimsy plastic ones, thought Miz Tiga disdainfully, as she poured the batter into the cake tin. Miz Tiga's fruitcakes were famous. She usually made several batches for Christmas, but this time, for want of condiments in her house to make bhang sherbet and laddus, she had decided to bake a cake.

Mr Tiga would have welcomed her cake, but of course he would have made sure the other sweets were there too. Mr Tiga was never one to be stingy on the table. All his friends said that. And Miz Tiga, once she learnt of her husband's weakness for a well-laid table, did her part with a zeal that earned her the loud appreciation of Mr Tiga's friends and the silent envy of their spouses.

'Miz Tiga!' he would call out. 'Miz Tiga, are you going to spend Holi in the kitchen? Then you better watch out! Here they are now, all ready to come in!'

Laughing, wiping her hands on the old sari worn especially for the colourful onslaught of Holi, Miz Tiga would emerge. Her half-hearted, feeble protests would be ignored and within minutes she would acquire green hair and a red and yellow face. Mr Tiga would grin back at her with a face that seemed dusted with the colours of the rainbow, his pristine white pyjama-kurta dyed a motley shade. Someone would bring out a dholak, someone else would bring out a harmonium, and lusty songs would be sung interrupted with shouts of *'Holi hai! Holi hai!'* The pitcher of bhang would be brought out. Steel tumblers would be passed around.

Plates of sweets would be served. The men would dance. The women would break out in uncontrollable giggles. Friends would come and go. The sun would climb higher in the sky, perhaps to get a better view of this raucously happy scene below. Nobody would feel the heat. They would be wet and cool, drenched from head to toe with coloured water.

Later on, when the shadows would start to grow long, the Tigas would laugh and go to Singh's house or to Tobias' house or to Roy's house, with their pressure cooker of khichri and tiffin box of fried vegetables; their contribution to an impromptu pot luck lunch. Nobody would mind that the khichri was cold, the fried vegetables soggy. The Tigas would not mind eating limp puris and congealed dum aloo. And, after that, tired and bleary-eyed, they would return home to bathe and freshen up for the evening. For Holi would not end there. It would end only after they joined their friends at the club where an old Hindi movie was screened and the club cook served up a hot dinner. And, after that, Mr and Miz Tiga would return home to the quarters of the company where Mr Tiga worked, the house in darkness because Miz Tiga for once would forget to switch on the porch light.

Miz Tiga sighed as she switched on the porch light. Fireflies were flitting about, puncturing little holes into dusk's violet sheet. The sounds of girls giggling reached out to her from what seemed to be an unbridgeable distance. This part of the school compound was the most silent. Mrs Bose was still with the girls, as were most of the other teachers and their families. A motley crowd was milling around the dining hall, the colours of Holi not quite gone from their faces and hair.

Miz Tiga lit a couple of mosquito coils. The smoke made her eyes water, but that was better than the buzzing little rascals. She sat on her rocker; her second cup of tea long grown cold beside her. The cake neatly sliced into thin squares lay quietly on the dining table inside.

'Miz Tiga?'

'Who is that?' said Miz Tiga squinting in the gloaming.

'It's me, Navjit, Miz Tiga.'

'So, you've come now! It's past dinner time, unless they are serving dinner late today!'

'They are serving dinner late today, because it's Holi, miss,' said the girl, inching timidly forward. 'Miss?'

'Yes, Navjit?'

'Happy Holi, miss.'

Miz Tiga got up and looked at the child. She was so thin and small, you could hardly believe that she was thirteen years old.

'Ha! You were the only one to remember your Miz Tiga, eh?'

'Yes, miss. I mean, no, miss. The other girls are a little busy, miss. I thought I'd come first, miss.'

'Hmm. No need to make excuses for those girls. I know all you girls like the back of my palm! Anyway, you come inside. I have something for you.'

Miz Tiga walked inside without bothering to see if the girl had followed. She put two slices of cake on a quarter plate and poured a orange squash in a glass from a tumbler.

'Come to the dining table and eat this,' she said gruffly.

The girl meekly sat down and ate with her head bowed. Miz Tiga watched her for a while. Then she packed the rest of the slices into a large steel tiffin box.

'Here,' she said. 'You take these back with you to the dining hall. Distribute them among the girls. Okay? Don't eat them by yourself.'

Navjit blinked. 'Yes, miss.'

She stood there awkwardly, holding the tiffin box. Her thin frame trembled a little as she struggled to say something.

'Miss?'

'Yes, what is it?'

'Miss, you are really very sweet, miss!' blurted Navjit.

Miz Tiga looked at Navjit for what seemed to be a very long time. Navjit was already wishing she had never opened her mouth.

'Hmmf! You remember to bring back my tiffin box tomorrow morning. Mr Tiga used to take his lunch in that.'

'Yes, miss. Thank you, miss,' said Navjit as she started to run back to her friends. 'Happy Holi again, Miz Tiga!'

'Happy Holi to all of you,' said Miz Tiga. But she said the words so softly, Navjit did not hear.

THE THIRTY-THIRD EGG

'*Ei*, Bhola! Late, again!' said Souvik.

Souvik was the head waiter at The Queen Victoria–Digha View Hotel, QVDV for short. He glared at Bhola. The fellow was tardy and careless. Souvik looked forward to the day when Bhola would get the boot. His nephew needed a job badly, and he needed a family member in the hotel to help him augment his under-the-table earnings.

'Fool! Watch the eggs,' he hissed before heading back to the kitchen.

Bhola acknowledged his boss with a barely perceptible nod. He slunk into his position behind the long buffet table where the breakfast was laid out. Diced papayas and watermelons, bunches of bananas, stacks of bread next to a toaster, small sachets of butter and jam, parathas, vegetable curry, fried potato wedges, cornflakes, savoury beaten rice, tea, coffee and jugs of hot milk. And, of course, eggs—hard-boiled and in their shells. The guests could also have eggs to order, but most didn't know or care. They were happy to pile two or three boiled eggs on to their plates whether they ate them or not.

It was past 7.30 a.m., and a few early risers were already queuing up at the buffet table. Bhola's eyes darted towards the egg pile. Nobody had touched them yet. But they would, he knew, at 8.30 a.m. Just the day before, the lady from Room No. 14 had dropped a dozen eggs straight into her handbag, right after she had put four on her own plate! A total of sixteen eggs at one go! A few of the guests had tittered. The lady had marched back to her table as regal as you please.

Bhola had ambled towards her table with a jug of water in his hand, as soon as he'd got an opportunity. Leaning forward, he had very respectfully whispered, '*Didimoni*, please, very very please. You eat as much here but please not keep eggs in handbag.'

The lady had glanced at him contemptuously, and thwacked an egg with the back of her spoon with such force that a piece of shell had flown out like a tiny odd-shaped saucer and landed on Bhola's lower lip.

'Don't tell me what I can or can't take. I am paying. You understand?' She hadn't even bothered to keep her voice down.

Gokul, the Odia boy who usually took food and drinks across to the rooms and also ran other errands for the hotel guests, gleefully reported seeing eggs in the dressing-table drawer of Room No. 14. The lady had even taken up a handful of salt mixed with pepper from the table wrapped in a paper napkin. She and her two friends had ordered vodka and lime cordial in the evening. When Gokul brought them up, he saw one of them hastily shutting the drawer, but not before he had seen the eggs and the shells.

'They ate the eggs for snacks with their vodka!' he announced to all and sundry in the kitchen.

A few staff members snickered. Some laughed outright. Some of them passed ribald comments. Only Bhola stood there like a stoic.

Souvik slapped him on the back of his head. 'It happened during your duty, you oaf. I'll make sure the cost of the eggs gets deducted from your salary.'

Bhola almost whimpered. Souvik always picked on him. It was not as if the guests didn't take more than they paid for when the others were on duty. But somehow his mistakes, and sometimes they were not even his own mistakes, were always noticed, reported to the manager, and at times blown out of proportion. He crept towards a corner of the kitchen. He scratched his head as he tried to calculate the amount to be deducted. One egg cost one rupee fifty paisa in the wholesale market. But Souvik, being a mean old fox, would deduct two rupees, and pocket the difference, he was certain. That was thirty-two rupees!

More than half a day's pay. Bhola, as a temporary staff, was paid on a per-day basis, with meals on the house.

Bhola licked a drop of tear that had rolled down his cheek. He would beg the lady in Room No. 14 to have mercy on him. He would press her legs if he had to. Surely, she, being a motherly type, would take pity on him? All plump, fifty-plus women appeared motherly to Bhola, including those who drank alcohol. His own mother was as thin as a stick and would have been horrified if she knew Bhola was serving alcohol to ladies. He hadn't seen her for many years. Bhola wiped his nose.

'Bhola!' barked Souvik. 'Stop staring at the wall! Duffer! Go deliver the soda and ice to Room No. 22.'

Room service was not really his job, but the boundaries were blurred for waiters. It was usually given to the smarter boys among the staff, and they earned a bit from the tips. Bhola picked up the tray and left. He would knock on Room No. 14's door once he had served the soda and ice to 22.

The tallest and slimmest member of the trio opened the door after his timid knock. Her spectacles shone like moonstones.

'We didn't call anyone,' she said.

'No, didi, I coming myself,' said Bhola. 'Please, small help. I must speak with other didi.' His heart hammered against his ribs.

'Which didi?'

'*Ke re*, Kakoli?' someone asked from inside, but it didn't sound like his didi, who he had mentally christened 'Dim-di' or egg-sister.

'A waiter, not sure which one of you he wants to speak to,' said Kakoli, without turning her head.

She left the door open and went inside. Bhola craned his neck as far as he could, but the small passage leading to the main room didn't offer any view. He heard the toilet being flushed, and the sound of a throat being cleared. The bathroom door opened. A rotund figure with a small towel draped on her nightie-clad shoulders emerged, and immediately let out a shriek.

'Ei! What is this? Who left the door open?' Bhola's Dim-di screamed.

'Don't scream, Dipa,' the two inside shouted in unison.

'It's that waiter,' said Kakoli.

'Must be the eggs,' said the other voice.

'Ei, Shonali, just keep shut,' said Dim-di. She looked at Bhola with red-rimmed eyes. 'Ki? What do you want?'

Bhola stood there with his hands folded into a namaste, and downcast eyes. 'Dim-d,' he bit his tongue and quickly corrected himself, 'Didimoni. Please. Saar taking my job away because of excess egg eating.'

'So? What can I do? Don't eat so many eggs if your job's at stake.'

Bhola shook his head. 'Not I eating the eggs, didimoni. Please, didi. I bringing good eggs at wholesale price for you,

55

personally boiled. No extra charging. Only wholesale cost of big-big eggs. White leghorn eggs, didimoni.' Tears stung Bhola's eyes. He was ready to fall at her feet.

The other two ladies came out.

'Can't you understand what he's saying, Dipa?' said Shonali. She appeared to be almost as wide as she was tall, an oblong pillar of muscle and fat. Bhola did not relish the idea of confronting her. His Dim-di looked comfortingly round and pleasing in comparison. Nevertheless, she seemed to be supporting him, so Bhola relaxed, but only a bit. 'The eggs you took will cost him his job.'

'What nonsense,' said Dipa, a little too quickly. She twisted the towel in her hands. 'Other guests take towels, pillows, cutlery . . . Arrey, even small items of furniture! What rot! I'm not paying for the eggs. Ei boy, you go. Don't act smart. I'll complain.'

Bhola sank to his knees, 'Please, didi. My boss not a good man. He saying he cutting salary for eggs. I am poor boy.'

'Why will he cut your salary when guests are eating the eggs?'

'Excess egg eating,' sobbed Bhola. 'I on duty for your table, didimoni. So, my salary cutting.'

'Oh, oh. Just get up, will you? Don't create a scene here.' Dim-di craned her neck to see if anyone loitering in the corridor had heard their conversation. Nobody was there. 'Ei, Kakoli, can you give this fellow ten rupees, please?' She said over her shoulder before returning her attention to Bhola. 'You go get vodka and lime cordial and ice, okay? Three glasses.'

'Ei na, I want gin today,' said Kakoli. She handed Bhola a ten-rupee note. 'Shonali, what about you?'

'Anything, anything,' said Shonali. 'Let's have it at the beach. Tell the fellow to take it to the deck chairs nearest our room, will you?'

'What's your name?' said Dipa.

'Bhola, didimoni.'

'Okay, listen Bhola. I'll give you some of the eggs. You get them sliced nicely. Put chopped onions, tomatoes, green chilli, coriander leaves, some lime juice and chaat masala, all right? Can you do that?'

Bhola nodded. He had the fascinated look of a man cast under a strong spell. Dipa looked regal and commanding. He had a sudden vision of her wearing a crown and the traditional white sholapith ornaments that Ma Durga wore when she was worshipped in the puja pandals. He assumed she belonged to an old zamindari family, and he wasn't far wrong. Dipa hurried inside and came out again with six eggs in a newspaper cone.

'I will know if the eggs are less,' she said. 'So, you make sure, okay? Tomorrow I'll give you another ten rupees. Now go get the drinks and egg chaat together,' she looked at him with big eyes. 'No hanky-panky. Be quick,' she added sternly.

Bhola took the cone of boiled eggs and raced down the corridor. His head buzzed. How on earth was he going to convince the kitchen boys to do the job? They might insist on billing the eggs. He would get into trouble with Dim-di if they did that. Perhaps he could raise a bill for the vegetable salad. Bhola stopped, struck by his own brilliance. Yes, of course. He would speak to Keshto-da, the head cook, directly, if he could avoid hawk-eyed Souvik. How he hated the man! But Keshto-da was kind. He would understand and not make a fuss about the salad. Bhola would quietly peel and slice the eggs and add them himself. Pleased with his idea, Bhola hurried back, and almost dashed into Souvik.

'Ass, where were you?' said Souvik barring Bhola's path.

'Taking order from No. 14 after delivering to 22.'

'Did they call you?'

'Uh, um. One didimoni saw me and told me.'

Souvik stared at him for a few seconds. 'What did they order?'

'Egg . . . No um, vegetable salad with chaat masala and lemon juice on top,' said Bhola, flustered by the slip of the tongue. 'And some coriander leaves,' he added to make up for the blunder.

'Hmm,' said Souvik. He had noted the egg bit. 'Those cheapskates will add the eggs they stole this morning to the salad. What else did they order? Vodka?'

'No, saar. Gin with lime cordial,' Bhola frowned to remember if there was anything else. His eyes lit up, 'Also, ice and soda.'

'Keshto, get one of the boys to make the salad for No. 14,' said Souvik, opening the door of the kitchen. He waved at Bhola with a careless hand. 'Follow me.'

Bhola went with him to the bar, and silently thanked the god or goddess who had looked out for him. Souvik had failed to notice the cone of eggs bulging out from Bhola's trouser-pocket.

Souvik measured three small pegs of Blue Riband Gin. He poured lime cordial into three shot glasses, and placed three soda bottles on the tray. 'Get the ice, tongs and paper napkins. Don't spill anything.'

Bhola nodded and picked up the laden tray. He went into the kitchen before collecting the ice. Keshto had chopped the vegetables himself, and the salad was almost ready. Bhola felt pleased. He set the tray down on the counter and slipped out to the rear side of the kitchen. This was the utility area, where the vessels and vegetables were washed, fish gutted and scaled and chickens plucked. The place was a mess, and quite filthy. Bhola cleared some space on the counter near the sink. He dug his hand into his pocket to retrieve the eggs. He peeled them quickly. A quick peep into the kitchen to see if Souvik was there— he was not—and Bhola returned to Keshto, a servile smile forming on his face.

'Keshto-da,' he simpered. 'Didi from 14 gave me the eggs to add to salad, please dada.'

Keshto didn't look up. He held out his left hand, palm side up. Bhola placed the cone of peeled eggs on it. Keshto sliced them quickly, arranged the vegetables and egg slices on an oval stainless-steel bowl, squeezed lemon juice and sprinkled coriander leaves. He scattered chaat masala, and handed it to Bhola. 'Cover it with paper napkins,' he said, without looking up. He did not give any indication of having noticed Bhola's deferential head nod.

Bhola put the covered salad on his tray and ran to the fridge to get ice. A small bowl of ice in hand, he turned and immediately froze in his tracks. Souvik had come in as silently as a snake and was about to lift the napkin off the salad bowl.

'Souvik da,' said Keshto calmly. 'Number 33 is vegetarian?'

'Vegetarian?!' said Souvik. 'They are Jains! No garlic, no onions!'

'Bengali widow's diet,' said Keshto grinning.

Keshto looked at his helpers. They tittered right on cue. Jokes began to be tossed about. Souvik took a swig from the glass he was holding. Everyone knew he pilfered from the bar and diluted the guests' liquor orders. Bhola saw his chance, and escaped with the salad and drinks.

The hotel staff always took the shortcut to the beach—a narrow alley between the two wings of the hotel. He paused to peer into the darkness as he emerged. The distant sounds of the Bay of Bengal, the smell of the salt water and the cool moist touch of a briny breeze made him feel hungry. He trudged through the hard sand in search of Dim-di and her two friends.

'Ei, ei, what's your name, this way!'

Bhola turned. He could make out whitish billowy shapes on some deck chairs. He hurried in that direction.

'You took a long time,' said Dipa, Bhola's Dim-di. 'Let me see the salad.'

'You and your eggs,' said Kakoli.

'Shush! *Chup kor,*' said Dipa. 'I've been an eggetarian all my life. And you know it.'

Shonali giggled, 'And you're egg-shaped as well.'

'What are you?' said Dipa, but without malice. 'A big fat slab of lard.'

'Bitch,' retorted Shonali cheerfully.

'Mind your language, girls,' said Kakoli.

'God! You still sound just like Sister Celia!' said Shonali.

'She was her chumchy in school, don't you remember?' said Dipa.

'Didimoni,' said Bhola, clearing his throat. 'Please sign here.' He bent down with the faux leather folder which held the bill.

'What's this?' said Dipa. 'I left my specs in the room. Someone read it, please.'

Kakoli peered at the paper under the light of her cell phone. 'It's the bill for a vegetable salad and another one for the drinks. Goodness! How much they charge here!'

'How much?' said Shonali and Dipa together.

'Arrey, two hundred and fifty rupees for the salad alone! And eight hundred for three gins with lime cordial?! Plus, taxes! This is robbery! They charged us the same for the vodka yesterday,' said Kakoli

'What is this?' said Dipa to Bhola. 'Why are you robbing us?'

'Didimoni, I not robber,' said Bhola. 'I only delivery man. Please sign this. Not pay, only sign. Before leaving hotel, you tell manager, please.'

'He's right,' said Shonali. 'Why yell at him? He's only serving.'

Bhola was relieved. He picked up the signed bills and hurried back. His duties didn't end until long past midnight. This was the peak season, and the demands of the guests were many. He served them in the dining hall, and took some trays to the rooms as well, because Gokul was overloaded. Afterwards, he managed a few morsels of dal and rice in the hotel kitchen before falling into a dreamless sleep in the small room he shared with five other hotel boys.

Sometime near dawn, bright light dazzled his eyes. Ma Durga, sitting on her lion, floated above him. The lion held a basket of eggs in his mouth. Ma Durga's spear had a giant egg attached to its pointy end. She began to prod Bhola with the egg-end of her spear.

'*Botso*,' she said, using the old Bengali word for boy. Her voice was exactly like Dim-di's, and so was her face. 'Botso, I have turned eggetarian. Offer me eggs, only nice big white leghorn eggs, from now on.'

Bhola knelt before her, one wary eye on the lion. 'Ma,' he said, 'I am your *bhokto*, your disciple. I will go to the ends of the earth and get the best leghorn eggs. The biggest I can find. Bless me, Ma Dugga.'

'I bless you, botso,' she said. 'Go forth and get me eggs. And I will grant you a boon.'

'Ma. Ma Dugga. Ma go,' mumbled Bhola. 'I will do your bidding, Ma Dugga.'

A sharp kick startled Bhola. He blinked.

'*Saala*!' said the roommate who slept next to his mattress on the floor. The others were snoring peacefully. 'We hardly get any sleep, and here you're chanting "Dugga Dugga"!'

'Sorry,' said Bhola, and turned over.

Bhola remembered the dream later in the day, at the breakfast buffet. Souvik had warned him about the eggs, so he counted them twice, and wrote the number down on a piece of paper. Dim-di and her friends arrived at nine. She slipped sixteen eggs at one go into her handbag, but didn't put any on her plate. Bhola loped towards their table.

'Dim-di,' he checked himself, shaking his head slightly as he bit his tongue. 'Didi, dim, please, you don't take so many. I will bring good eggs for you. Please.'

Dipa looked at him with large round eyes. The whites of her eyes gleamed like leghorn eggs. Her hair was wet and hung in long loose curls about her face. The morning sun touched her cheeks with a rosy glow. Bhola was transfixed. She was Ma Durga, no doubt about it.

'We are leaving this afternoon. I will need the eggs for dinner. Why are you afraid? I said I'll give you ten rupees.'

'Dugga. Dugga,' he chanted in his head, before bending his head to whisper just loud enough for her to hear, 'Souvik head waiter, didi, very angry.'

'I will tell him not to be angry with you,' she said calmly before returning to her parathas and curry. 'Get me some coffee.'

Souvik refused to believe she had taken sixteen eggs.

'Liar. I'll have you sacked!' he shouted. 'I counted the eggs myself. Seventeen are missing today, unaccounted for. I know who ate the eggs and how many. Your Room 14 took thirty-two eggs in total. In two days! Saala! Where is the thirty-third egg? Who took it today?'

'I didn't saar,' said Bhola and immediately received a cuff on his ear.

The hullabaloo brought the manager into the kitchen. The staff stood quietly around, waiting for what they each secretly feared to unfold.

'Saar, you don't know,' said Souvik, immediately turning servile. 'This Bholaram here is a number-one scoundrel. The drinks are diluted. The eggs go missing. The Bombay mixture and peanuts get finished too quickly! Here's your culprit!'

'No, saar,' said Bhola. Tears rolled down his cheeks. 'No, saar.'

Souvik cuffed his ear again. 'No, saar! Huh! Acting innocent now?!'

'See me in my office,' said the manager to Bhola and left.

Souvik smirked triumphantly.

The minute he left, Keshto pushed a plate with three parathas and a good helping of curry towards Bhola.

'Eat this before you go to the manager,' he said, adding gruffly. 'That rascal Souvik is bringing his nephew to work here. It's an open secret. He just needed a scapegoat.'

Bhola had no appetite. But he ate. He didn't know when or where or how he would be able to eat next. The manager turned out to be kinder than Souvik. He didn't deduct the price of the thirty-three eggs from his salary. But with his job gone, this was small comfort. Bhola picked up his meagre belongings from the room. He went to the ocean's edge and sat there for a long time. His mind was blank. He even nodded off for a minute or two. The sun, now high up in the sky, cast an orange brightness on his closed eyelids. Ma Durga's face swam into view. Bhola jerked his head up. Dugga, Dugga! He knew exactly what he had to do.

His reasoning was straightforward. Whether she had meant to or not, Dim-di was responsible for his job loss. She was also a good person. She would not have come to him in his dreams as Ma Dugga if she weren't. Buoyed up by the thought, Bhola got up and ran back towards the hotel. The doorman told him that the three ladies had just come down and were having a heated argument over the bill with the manager. Their ride was waiting. He pointed to a cream-coloured Innova standing among other cars in the hotel's parking area. The driver lay almost supine on the reclined driver's seat. Bhola walked up to him.

'Dada,' he said gently tapping the window. 'Dada, where is didimoni going?'

The driver opened his eyes. 'Rashbehari Avenue.'

'How long will it take?'

'Four and a half hours; why?'

'I have to go also, but by bus. Dada, you have exact address of didimoni?'

The driver looked at him quizzically. 'Arrey, it's the Ghosh Bari, haven't you heard of it? Old Kolkata family. They have a Durga puja every year. Large red house.' He looked into his rear-view mirror. 'Here they come.' He straightened up his seat and turned on the AC. Bhola stood aside waiting.

'Oh look, our waiter has come for his ten rupees,' said Kakoli.

Shonali tittered.

'No need for sarcasm,' said Dipa. She was cross because the argument with the manager hadn't gone too well. Kakoli had made too many snide remarks and the manager had turned, Dipa felt, disrespectful. Shonali was useless when it came to crunching numbers. It was left to Dipa to try and strike a bargain. She wasn't satisfied with the results. And now they were about to be ambushed by the waiter.

'What do you want?' said Dipa.

'Didimoni, I lost my job,' said Bhola and immediately began to wipe his eyes. 'Eggs,' he managed to say in between sniffs.

'Good god!' said Shonali. 'What a cheap hotel!'

'Hotel is fine. It's the manager,' said Kakoli.

'No didimoni, it is that head waiter, Souvik,' said Bhola darkly. 'He is always stealing. And now he wants to give my job to his nephew. So, he got me kicked out. Using egg as excuse.'

The three ladies stared at him.

'Because of eggs?' said Kakoli. She looked at Dipa. 'Your responsibility,' she said and got into the car.

'Why my responsibility?' said Dipa frowning. 'All of us ate the eggs.'

'Not all,' said Kakoli. Her spectacles glinted in the sun. 'You've got sixteen of them, hard-boiled and all, in your luggage waiting to be turned into dinner.'

Shonali giggled.

'Shonali, don't laugh,' said Dipa. 'You two are staying over for the night, so don't tell me the eggs are my responsibility alone.'

'I'm only having boiled potato, rice and ghee for dinner. Three days of hotel food has turned my stomach,' said Kakoli. She had taken off her spectacles and was putting on a pair of large dark glasses.

'Boiled egg is good with potato, rice and ghee,' said Shonali, and giggled again.

'Shonali, stop it,' said Dipa. 'You,' she said turning towards Bhola. 'What do you want?'

'Ten rupees,' said Shonali. Her shoulders shook with laughter. She almost collapsed into her seat.

'Eggs,' said Kakoli, laughing. 'Give him back the eggs.'

Dipa tried to silence her friends with a gesture. She fished out her wallet from her handbag. 'I'll give you twenty rupees, okay?'

'Didi, can you give me a job?' said Bhola. His desperation had made him bold.

'What?!'

'Please, didimoni,' said Bhola. 'I have widow mother at home. Three sisters to marry off. Father dead. I sole earner. Please help.' His eyes became wet again. He had spoken with such earnestness that his story seemed to ring true even to his own ears.

'What job can I give you?' said Dipa.

'I can cook,' said Bhola eagerly. The spark in Dipa's eyes gave him hope. 'Eggs, many kinds of eggs.'

Kakoli and Shonali nudged each other and giggled. Dipa remained serious. She needed a cook. Desperately. But she didn't know the fellow. What if he turned out to be a thief? Bhola saw her hesitate, and decided to drive home his cooking skills.

'Egg chop, egg curry, egg *kosha*, egg *bhurji*, egg omelette, egg korma, egg mustard steamed, egg mustard gravy, egg poach, egg fry, egg omelette *jhaal*, egg omelette gravy with tomato, egg half-boil, egg full-boil, egg French toast, egg sweet French toast,' he rattled off the list like he was reading a menu card.

Shonali and Kakoli went into splits. Even their driver began to smile. Dipa frowned as she pondered over the idea.

'You can come with us,' she said at last. Bhola was about to touch her feet, but she stopped him. 'I will first test you at home and then see. Of course, I will give you return fare if you don't get the job.'

'Yes, *maiji*,' said Bhola. Now that she was a prospective employer, he felt it was better to elevate her to maiji from didimoni. He hurried forward to sit next to the driver.

'Really, Dipa,' said Kakoli. 'You are the pits!'

'No risks taken, no battles won,' said Dipa philosophically. She delved into her handbag for her sunglasses and brought out an egg. 'Good god, how did this get in here?'

'Oh my god!' shrieked Shonali. Her face turned red. Her body shook with helpless laughter.

'Dipa, you put sixteen in your luggage and one in your bag?' Kakoli spluttered. 'This is the height!'

'Oh my god!' said Shonali again. 'Oh my god!' She looked ready to burst, but sobered up after a minute. 'Don't eggs bring bad luck when you're travelling?'

'Superstition!' said Dipa, cupping the egg in her hand. 'Plain superstition. Boiled egg is the best, cleanest, most nutritious food you can take with you when travelling.' She paused, looking at her egg in puzzlement. 'Believe me, I don't remember taking this one though. Wonder how it got in my bag.'

Sitting upright in the front seat and clutching his cloth bag as he watched the road rolling back beneath the now fast-moving car, Bhola kept a straight face. His offering to Ma Dugga had borne fruit. Almost immediately. He was a content man. And a positively grateful one. Bhola closed his eyes to get a clearer vision of his special egg-loving deity, she who had blessed him earlier that day.

'Dugga, Dugga,' he whispered, 'Joy Baba Bigneswar.' This was the auspicious mantra one chanted before the start of any journey. But Bhola kept chanting it to himself intermittently, all the way to Kolkata.

THE AMMA WHO
TOOK FRENCH LEAVE

Amma had never done anything like this before. She was a good sort. She was honest and did her job with sincerity. Aditi had never had any trouble from her before. No sloppy work. No tardiness. No stealing the odd handful of rice or potatoes. No complaints of drunken husbands or sons. Amma's work was clean, and she arrived on time every day. On top of that, she never took a Sunday off. Not one. Aditi considered her a godsend in a place where it was impossible to survive without maids. One had no choice but to depend on them here, the way one depended on the very water of life. Aditi had learnt that soon enough, after her return.

Aditi had learnt a lot of other things too since then, and relearnt a few old housekeeping lessons as well, taught by her mother during her girlhood. Vital housekeeping lessons, like how homes here needed to be cleaned every day, even twice a day, with the good old dust cloth, rice-stalk broom, a rag and pail of water. Here, steel vessels had to be shone with steel wool and coarse grainy soap. Vegetables had to be presoaked and then washed in running water again and again. Rice needed to be picked clean of grit and then washed and washed until the water ran clear. Drinking water had to be bought for seventy rupees for a twenty-five-litre can. Aditi had to unlearn her habit of drinking straight from the tap. She also had to unlearn a few more things she had picked up in the US, like walking around her home in outdoor shoes instead of changing into rubber flip-flops, and leaving the bread in the bread bin. The roads were so dirty that it was a sacrilege to walk around the house in shoes. As for the bread, it quickly turned mouldy outside the refrigerator.

Aditi, nonetheless, soon began to appreciate that here, a harried homemaker could get someone to wash and rinse her cup of mid-morning coffee long after the morning's cooking vessels were cleaned. Here there was someone to rub soothing oil into one's aching scalp. Here a woman could have that other woman in her life to share the burden of housekeeping with. Perhaps that was why these women were called 'amma' or mother. Naturally, Aditi could hardly be blamed for feeling angry and betrayed when her Amma disappeared, just like that, for one whole week!

As maids go, she was rare. Aditi knew it. Her neighbours knew it. Maybe one of them had wooed her with a bigger salary? Neighbours were known to do worse in these parts. Maybe Amma had decided to leave all of a sudden. Maids were known to do that. It was the quality of their lives. It made them a little crazy in the head. Heaven knew what went on in that wizened old head of hers! So far, she'd been quite reliable. Aditi had got used to her unassuming ways. She had actually begun to believe that at least her Amma was loyal—definitely better than the rest.

Amma didn't give any warning, not even a hint. Aditi wasted the first day waiting for her to turn up. Then, for the next two days, she did Amma's job, tiring herself out and looking like a frump in the process. It was hard work, now that she had grown used to a maid's services all over again. In the US, she'd had little choice. But the housework got done faster there, with all the machines and ready-made food items. Her husband used to help too. But now, he had returned to his pampered old self, and had even employed a man to clean his car every day for a salary of two-hundred rupees a month! He complained of the lack of disciplined traffic and poor quality of service—'they'll work for peanuts and work like monkeys!' was his favourite complaint. He fumed about the general tardiness everywhere. So, he went late to office, because no one came on time, and returned late, sometimes at eleven in the night, because everyone worked 'lazily'. Of course, he never had time to even talk to Aditi, let alone help her with housework. He gave her a chauffeured car, so she could do the grocery shopping on her own, or go out where she liked. But where could one go? One couldn't eat at a restaurant nor go to the beach for a jaunt or to the movies alone. That left only the shopping malls, which left Aditi feeling nostalgic and outraged, because Indian prices seemed steeper than what she was accustomed to for the same things back in the US.

Aditi felt like screaming. She didn't, of course. What would the neighbours say? Instead, she stoically went about cooking and cleaning. As if she had a choice! Nobody would come. Nobody would want to do a temporary job, unless it was one of Amma's friends. But Aditi's Amma sent neither word nor substitute. She did nothing. Nobody knew where she'd gone. And as the days passed, Aditi felt more and more depressed and unloved, like a martyr ignored. So, what did Amma expect? Aditi had to find another Amma. And she did.

The new one seemed alright so far. She charged more because she could speak a little English. Aditi didn't mind shelling out the extra money. The new Amma's knowledge of English, however scanty, had made it so much easier. The old Amma and Aditi would communicate mostly in sign language. She found it frustrating when she wanted Amma to clean a spot that she'd missed or tell her to handle the crystal with care when she dusted the tables and shelves. Now all that was comfortably in the past. Or so Aditi thought until she answered the door one morning, at the exact time her old Amma used to ring the bell.

It was indeed Amma, back like the prodigal returned. Possibly to reclaim her job. Blinking behind her spectacles owlishly, she stood before Aditi with her withered hands rising in supplication. Aditi spoke no Tamil, so the watchman had to translate. She listened to the old Amma's plea. Amma wanted Aditi to excuse her absence, the French leave that she took. It was a stampede, she explained via the watchman, a stampede of impatient humans at a school. There were at least a hundred people, rushing forward to claim the food and clothes that ended up claiming the lives of her boys. The youngest, her grandson, was just twelve.

What stampede and what school was she talking about? Aditi asked her through the watchman. The watchman, a hoary old fellow, with a disapproving face and servile posture, said that family members of tsunami victims were being given compensation of rice and clothes by a charity organization. But the tsunami occurred years ago, Aditi exclaimed. What kind of a cock and bull story was this?

The watchman was quiet for a minute. Amma stood still, incomprehension writ large on her face. The watchman, a note of weary patience slowing down his words, spoke again, swallowing back a tobacco-flavoured spittle of bitterness.

The tsunami victims still needed help, he told Aditi. Many of them were yet to receive compensation. Many of them hadn't been able to move into new homes. The houses hadn't been built yet. Many more waited to be allotted new houses. They were living in makeshift dwellings, patched together from discarded tarpaulin, plastic sheets and thatch; they were trying to make ends meet with the remnants of their families and friends.

The watchman did not bother to ask why Aditi was not aware. They were living in the same country after all, same city in fact. He said nothing that came close to impertinence. But the questions stood there before Aditi, beating a tattoo of accusation on her door.

Aditi had nothing to say. Of course, she had read all about it in the newspapers, but hadn't given it much thought. Their world and hers were so far apart. She had her own set of problems, just as they had theirs. Life here was no cakewalk, despite the glitter of global-cuisine restaurants and shimmering malls. Besides, it hadn't occurred to Aditi that her Amma could be involved. That she was a part of *them*.

Now that she'd heard about it, Aditi felt genuinely sorry for her. And genuinely helpless too. She could feel as guilty as she wanted, but she couldn't throw out the other Amma for no reason. Could she? That would be unfair too. Would her old Amma understand the predicament?

The watchman looked at Amma without speaking. Amma sighed before nodding in that strange neither-yes-nor-no-way to show that she did understand. Aditi's predicament transcended all language barriers. Her old Amma and her new. They were after all sisters from the same tribe. They would not grudge each other's bread. Their stories could be different, but their sorrows were the same. Their separate lives were stitched together like a patchwork quilt with the same thread of hard truth running between the cloth pieces.

Aditi's old Amma seemed to know instinctively that one job lost was only one meal lost in a day. She told Aditi so, through the watchman's surly lips. It was alright. Her old limbs would have that extra time to rest. An old woman needed more rest than food. She fell silent again. A wobbly parenthesis hovered outside Aditi's door. She stood there lost in her thoughts and memories. Aditi observed her searching for something in the sunlight. There was no anger or reproach in her eyes. But Aditi's awkwardness returned nevertheless. She didn't know how long she could stand this.

The Amma looked up at Aditi and the watchman translated again. Now that Amma had no one, now that she no longer had to save for her grandson's education, her life felt like an empty gourd.

Aditi looked away. It was near impossible to fill her heart up with this truth. She could not bear Amma to speak about her present life. Aditi thrust some five-hundred-rupee notes into her hands. They were crisp and new; more than Amma's monthly salary. Aditi released the notes into the Amma's bent and damp hands, and the rustle of the paper dissolved into silence.

Aditi knew that this was small compensation for the three lives that were snuffed out. She still could not bear to look at her. But Amma accepted the notes. Aditi felt relieved. She didn't have to elaborate any more on why she had taken in the substitute Amma.

The old Amma apologized again for not sending word. It had happened so fast, she said. She had to identify her losses through the slippers they had lost. She had to get the bodies out of the sun as fast as she could. She had to arrange the triple funeral quickly, very quickly, for the sun pours his wrath on all, without exception. Just like the sea. She murmured to herself without rancour. The watchman interpreted her without pity. Aditi flinched at every word she was made to hear. And then, Amma fell silent again. Her grief cutting a deep trench across which the words could not spill over. Aditi could see how sharply it had etched into her bones, till it no longer showed up in her eyes.

Abruptly, the old Amma left, leaving a breath heaving in mid-air.

The watchman turned too, and marched back to his post by the main gate, his shadow crouching like an angry

Quasimodo beneath his corny feet. Aditi returned indoors to confront her new Amma's eyes.

They searched hers. It didn't take the new Amma long to find what she was looking for. There was a look of relief in them that worked on Aditi's scalp like thin work-calloused fingers, propelling her head the other way.

Aditi looked at other things. She watched a fly settle on the ceiling. She sat with the newspaper opened, spread out on the dining table. She scanned the news, but saw the old Amma in the newsprint instead. She saw her wrinkles. She imagined them bearing the weight of bodies. She saw her old Amma collecting faggots beneath trees; faggots for her three pyres.

Aditi saw the edge of Amma's blue sari flying above her head like a kite, fluttering to free itself from the clutches of twiggy branches. Amma wore recycled tyre slippers, clutched tight below her toes, clawing the soil hard beneath her feet. She had a one-litre bottle of kerosene in her hands. She had bought the fuel from the black market, because there was no time to queue up before the ration shop for the government's fair-price kerosene. Aditi could smell the flames crackling over the dry skin of lives that a giant wave of water killed years after it had receded back into the ocean's belly. Aditi sat at her dining table, and tasted the sticky ash of burnt flesh in her coffee.

Aditi drew the curtains and shut her doors to the dust and itinerant vendors outside. She settled into her chair again. She returned to her coffee, now fragrant again, and to the crossword in the newspaper. The day started to become ordinary again. Her mind settled down among the running sands of her orderly days, pecking about its small details like a busy hen. A frown gathered upon her forehead. Practical things began to probe and question, trying to make sense of her impulsive generosity. And Aditi picked up the pen, her hand poised over a scrap of paper. She sipped her coffee and turned to work out the week's housekeeping accounts again, now that she was a few five-hundred-rupee notes short.

LID BANGED SHUT

The thought lands without warning. Just like Meera's one-eyed tomcat, which has the habit of dropping soundlessly from the garden wall, casually interrupting the quietness of a day about to curl up for the night. The sun is already sliding down a livid sky, and shades of the evening are gathering around her. Romola drags on the cigar. It's one of the stubs she saved before Dillip died.

'What's the big idea?' she muses. 'Thirty years of married life spent with two husbands in close succession, and then the lovers. And the children, all six of them.' The thought of love makes her snort, and then cough, as the cigar fumes sting her lungs.

Meera, of course, would have swept it all away. Romola involuntarily shakes her head. Meera could be as indignant as she wanted, but how could Romola have known love when she had never loved anyone? At least, not in that heart-fluttering, leaky-bladder kind of way. There was also that gut-wrenching sensation of belonging, to a man, a place; the shared emotions and memories. Romola had seen it in the movie rendition of *Gone with the Wind*, shining like twin green beacons from Scarlett O'Hara's eyes as she stood before the ruins of her beloved Tara.

'Now *she* had a man who knew a thing or two about love,' she mutters, and draws some more on the smouldering stub. What she herself had experienced was a purely physical thing, instinctive, almost animal-like. 'Romance? Heart candy, that's what!' And the smoke almost belches out of her nostrils.

Romola had never been the archetypal wife and mother, the simpering lover. Her men, during her younger days, had been as much attracted to her beauty as they were to her biting intelligence. Her children looked up to her; Meera had told her so, over and over again.

Romola spits out a fleck of tobacco over the railing. Is there a note of mockery in the chirping of the sparrows in the rafters? She can't be sure. The pesky birds are still there and so are their untidy nests. No matter how many times she's got the gardener to smash their homes and eggs, the birds have returned. Now their preening feathers catch the gold from the setting sun's rays. Romola tilts her head to see better, but the sun has already blurred into a shapeless mass of lurid colours. The smoke uncurls and wafts into the garden.

Dillip would smoke cigars only till they were halfway through, sometimes even less. He would lay them down on an ashtray, only to light up a fresh one, often mere minutes later. The first time Romola saw him do it, she picked up the half-smoked cigar (in a moment of weakness, she told herself later) wrapped it in cellophane tightly and placed it in a carved rosewood jewellery box. Dillip had been surprised, and amused. Nevertheless, after that day, Dillip had begun arriving home from work with a fistful of partially smoked cigars. Romola had received them silently. She had pinched out the burnt parts, wrapped the cigars in cellophane, and stored them. Her collection had grown too big to be housed in a jewellery box. Dillip had got her a large wooden chest carved with intricate Kashmiri designs, its interiors scattered with little silken bags of desiccants. Years later, when Dillip lay dying of cancer, he had looked in the direction of the chest in their bedroom and smiled.

Patting Romola's hand, he had whispered, 'I'll be there, in the cigars for you. Always.'

After that, Romola took to smoking his cigars, once in a while at first, and more frequently after the children grew up. She did not attempt to understand why. That was simply not her style.

Dillip had certainly deserved her love. Even though he had never been a demonstrative man, his lovemaking had been more intense than the watery embraces of her first husband. Besides, she already had her lovers by then. Dillip had never outwardly shown any jealousy. There were times when she felt that Dillip had married her for reasons she would never be able to fathom completely, that he had married her not because of, but in spite of, her beauty and accomplishments—she was a 'fine student of grace and refinement', that was what her first husband used to say when people complimented her, and she was, to use his own words, 'the Venus de Milo that he had brought to life'.

Romola had already become an 'accomplished work of art'—another one of her first husband's cherished phrases—when Dillip came into her life. Yet, Romola felt that she hadn't quite passed the final test as far as he was concerned. He seemed to know the exact shape of her mind. Suspicion gnawed at Romola's heart. She felt like a performer in an ongoing play whose exclusive and sole spectator bore into the very essence of her being. It had not been possible to love Dillip with the abandon that the word craved. But he had been a good husband. He had been the respite from her lovers that she welcomed, like boiled rice and potatoes after a string of dinner parties which always had the same deep-fried fare trying hard to dress up as continental. She used to enjoy the occasional British colonial cuisine though. Kedgeree was a favourite, and so was crème caramel.

Romola's breasts don't quite muster the pencil test, but they don't flap like pelicans' beaks under her brassiere either, unlike Meera's. Romola's hair is now the colour of burnt coal, when it once flowed like an ebony river. Her gold-flecked green eyes now have a thin rim of grey, the first signs of cataract. And her dimples are less deep, though still charming. She looks at the pleats on her knuckles for a fleeting moment before crushing the cigar stub.

In that instant, a mere split second of a summer dusk, when the sun seems to have had too much to drink and simply can't get up and call it a day, and everything else is bathed with quiet gold. And it races ahead like a series of split-second-long television soap operas.

It's enough to leave her feeling drained, as if a plug has been pulled out from somewhere within. She shivers as a sudden chill wraps itself around her. And she wonders if anyone else has ever guessed what lies within her heart, even though she has never guessed it before herself. Dillip must have. The thought rises and sinks again, leaving a buoy of doubt bobbing in her head.

Meera would call them a poster couple. Romola smiles. Thank god for loyal, affectionate, happy and mundane Meera. Meera who dotes on her children, and they, on her. Even Dillip, who was generally polite and aloof with other women, would treat her with affection. Romola's life would have been far less exciting without Meera to take care of everyday matters. It seemed like Meera had always been there for Romola and her family. In reality though, the small cottage next door (an overlooked part of their large property, and Romola had barely had time to even think about it let alone ask Dillip) had lain vacant for nearly three years after Dillip and she moved into their home. Those first years had been difficult. Romola had struggled to keep her sanity with two children from her first marriage, and a third, Dillip's, on the way. Despite the retinue of help, mostly British-trained and newly unemployed as India gained Independence, Romola felt herself growing torpid, sapped of charm and wit, the two qualities that had first drawn Dillip towards her. Then Meera arrived, with her cats and a cage bursting with budgerigars. A commonplace friendship between the pregnant Romola and the bustling Meera began. Soon after, the two children were sucking their thumbs with rapt attention as Meera was narrating stories after stories. The cook began to produce full-course meals without mishap; the maid remembered to soak Romola's swollen feet in a tub of warm water; the gardeners trimmed the hedges and lawns—in short, her home started to hum efficiently. And Romola, at last, began to feel like a true mistress of her house.

Within two years of Meera's ministrations, Romola became beautiful, vivacious and irresistible all over again. Unshackled from the drudgery of motherhood, Romola regained her figure and charm, even after the last of her six children was born. Dillip, always a busy man and grown busier over the years, apologized for his absence by showering her with expensive gifts—a chauffeured car, jewellery and money.

Romola was a little wary at first. Meera seemed too good to be true. Then one day, when Romola lay on her bed with a fever, Meera walked in unannounced. She put cold compresses on her forehead, stroked her then jet-black hair and pressed the balls of her feet. Romola could not flinch away from the compassion in her touch. A new intimacy developed between them. Meera became the pillar upon which Romola's firmament stayed aloft.

There had been many men in Romola's life, and each was like an individual story in a book of short stories. She liked to look back at the closed chapters and to reimagine the episodes differently, even apply the new techniques freshly learnt from the past to the latest developing chapter. The one common thread running through all her love stories was that all her men had money. Her secret collection of jewellery could testify to that. But Romola had given back as well. She had been worth it.

Romola's children inherited her looks and elegant disposition. Now all, but one, are grown up with homes and families of their own. The children visit every year on Dillip's death anniversary. Romola's house fills up like a Christmas stocking when they come, bulging with conversation and laughter and the warm aroma of food. Meera has become a permanent fixture, with the children's children trailing after her like a wedding train. Meera loves the gatherings. The children and their children love Meera back. They sit together in the cosy second parlour after dinner, with Meera rocking in Dillip's chair, while Romola's children tell the little ones stories of their childhood spent with Meera.

Romola sees her youngest, thin and boyish even at twenty, and prone to pondering in the garden, often by starlight, returning. He is neither a poet, nor inclined to paint. His silences are that of a philosopher. Romola watches him ambling up the porch steps. She calls out to him and he stops briefly in response.

'Dinner's ready,' she says. 'And afterwards we could . . .'

He doesn't wait for her to finish. 'Thank you, mother, I ate at Meera *mashi*'s.'

Meera 'mashi'. Mother's sister. How easy it was for a woman's friend to become that to her children. Meera. Swarthy Meera with chipped teeth and dull wiry hair. She brings with her the wholesome goodness of dal-roti, and the pleasant breeze of utter dependability.

Romola flicks off the cigar ash. Meera may as well have been part of Romola's trousseau. Just like the brides of old zamindar families who brought a trusted maid with them along with their dowries. Wasn't that what Dillip had said once, when he chanced upon them while Meera was braiding Romola's hair? There had been something in his tone that she hadn't been able to put a finger on. Meera, of course, had smiled good-naturedly and left. She had returned with a tray of cups of tea and snacks, and quietly left again. But the air had quavered between them that evening. And afterwards Romola had felt the need to do something. Give Meera a token of her friendship. Her turquoise locket. And Meera held it precious, next to her bosom on a thin gold chain, always. Romola never wore turquoise jewellery again, even though it was one of her favourite stones.

Romola feels an urge to talk to her son. She wants to know what he has seen in the stars that are now visible. Has he seen a new star? Or has he seen an old star in a new light? These days she aches to speak with her children, about things that interest them, not just mundane things. She craves to see what their worlds are like, and he is the only one left. But the boy has already gone in.

Romola gets up to follow him. On her way up, as she crosses the second parlour, she hesitates. The carved wooden chest that houses her cigar stub collection, and increasingly these days, fresh cigars as well, stands in its corner by the window. She had got the servants to bring it down from her bedroom upstairs, because she mostly smoked on the porch. The cigar smell that lingered in her bedroom curtains had started to turn acrid in her nostrils. Once she'd woken up with a heavy feeling in her chest, as if a feral beast was sitting on it. She had the room thoroughly aired out the next day, and shifted the cigar chest downstairs.

Romola enters the room and opens the chest again. She can smoke one last cigar before retiring. The very last run of sunlight falls on the royal blue brocade curtains giving them the sheen of turquoise. The room looks rich and mysterious. As if it has withheld a bit of itself from her during these years, just like that sudden turquoise shade.

Romola lets the lid fall back with a bang. She walks back to the porch and down the steps. She takes a shortcut through her garden to Meera's cottage. The sun has vanished behind the Kanchenjunga. The embers of light left behind lead Romola down the flagstoned path to Meera's kitchen. She stands on her toes and taps on the windowpane. Meera peers out, frowning. After a while she recognizes her and cries out in surprise. She flings the kitchen door open and almost runs out into the backyard. Light from the kitchen and the bulb hanging above the door fall on her squat frame. Her smile is guileless, and so large it is almost a grin.

Romola gazes at her. Meera looks like a woman who has never been disappointed before. A woman who expects nothing untoward to happen to her. One whose life has been smooth and predictable, and as still as well water.

Meera's tomcat jumps in from the dark and stands at Meera's feet, almost like a guard, tail raised, but not at Romola. Startled, Romola stumbles a few steps backwards. Meera is quick to extend her hand. The tomcat now lowers its tail and swishes it, watching Romola intently. Reaching for Meera's hand, Romola sees the slim gold ring that she always wears on her ring finger. Light winks off its smooth surface. The ring, pale against careworn skin, seems as much a part of Meera as the turquoise locket around her neck. Romola stares at the ring until all she sees is its halo. Words that had risen to mind sink back like stones into her heart. She has seen the ring almost every single day of their decades-long relationship, yet she has never known it. Now it is there before her, clear and true.

How arrogant she has been, and how naïve and foolish? Love? Yes, indeed, what did she even know of love, and all its insidious, secret ways? Her affairs had been nothing, nothing compared to this. If anything, they had been a result of her unconscious need for love.

Romola stands, not moving, not blinking; seeing nothing but Meera's finger with the gold band. Stray conversations, quiet laughter, bodies held at angles that would have revealed something to the one whose sight was unclouded. All these mementoes crowd behind her in the dark. What if Dillip had still been alive at this very hour? What if he was smoking his post dinner cigar on the porch? Would she have run back to confront him? A length of ice-cold wire encircles her heart.

'She's even got my children!' And Romola can't push the thought away. She needs her strength to stop the tears. But Meera is still smiling. Compassionately. So Romola returns the smile. Even as the ring on Meera's finger seems to float up, mocking her, the sun in an eclipse through which she can see her past life, lengthening behind her like the scaly extent of a smoked out, burnt-to-ashes cigar.

MARITAL BLISS

Do I love Hem? Had this question been part of a questionnaire in which I had to choose one of three answers, namely 'yes', 'no' and 'not applicable', I would have ticked the last. Hem and I have been married long enough for boredom to lie between us like the third bedfellow. Together we have reached life's midstream; too far to jump out and swim either way. Even so, our marriage is going strong, like a balsa wood raft on a swiftly flowing river. There are times though when Hem makes me want to duck his head under water.

Both Hem and I look young despite our forty-plus years. Both my children are proud that I look much younger than their friends' mothers, which is nice, but I believe in being practical. Comfort before looks, I always say. I use reading glasses. On the other hand, Hem, who has large soulful eyes with long lashes, squints when he drives and watches TV from almost an inch away from the screen, but won't go to the ophthalmologist. Well, each man to his own vanity, which in Hem's case, also includes his idiosyncrasies. For my dear husband always remembers his own birthday, but never mine or even the children's; he will watch an entire movie with rapt attention, even get irritated if we sneeze, and then forget it completely as soon it is over; he gets hyper when he discovers randomly kept shoes on the rack but never remembers to pick up his dirty clothes after returning home from work. The list is a story by itself, hotly denied by Hem, my investment-banker husband, who spends long hours at his computer table both at office and at home and does not have too many interests outside his work, despite my efforts. Another thing Hem has very little interest in is the game of golf. He plays it nonetheless, partly because most of his clients do, and partly because it makes me happy. Hem feels constipated without the newspaper with him in the bathroom and reads only thrillers for entertainment. Hem, however, does have one real weakness—he loves assembling model airplanes and ships. It is his all-consuming passion.

I don't have too many interests and hobbies either. My family, my home, it's the only profession and interest or passion that I have. My dishes are famous, my house looks like we spent a fortune on an interior designer, when in reality, it is all my imagination and sourcing talent, and I make sure everyone in my family looks good. I always tell Hem when a suit does not flatter him or a little gob is sticking out from his nostril hairs. I believe it's a wife's duty to ensure that her husband is well turned out, right down to the fresh and hole-free socks beneath the gleaming shoes on his feet. It is always the small things that give people away. Hem is always well-fed, his clothes are always well-pressed, his bills are always paid, his children are always ahead in class and his wife, that is me, is always the one his friends wish they had married instead!

His friends' wives (actually, I should say *our* friends' wives!) bitch about me; at least most of them do. From those that don't (these are the ones who have some accomplishment to their credit, like Sheena who is a pilot, or Paula who is a hotshot lawyer) I get subtle reminders that I am a housewife while they have a status beyond being so-and-so's wife. Just to give you an example, the other day, with platters piled high with all the exotic and not-so-exotic but delectable hors d'oeuvres that I had taken such pains to create for the party we were throwing, Paula said huskily for all ears around us, 'Oh Tara, you're so good at all this stuff, I wish I had the *time* to be like you!'

Another time, when I met them at Hem's office party, during an animated discussion about politics or economics, (who cares, I just like to be where the action at a party is happening), Sheena turned to me even before I had arranged my torso in the right posture and said, 'Hem is a lucky man. He can sleep in peace, knowing his wife is right next to him, and not flying a plane that could be shot down or hijacked!'

Always the sport, Hem, tried to carry the joke a little further, 'Sheena, your Shekhar is the lucky guy! Not I.'

Sheena punched him playfully; everybody laughed, including me, because I am always graceful. Afterwards, Shekhar whispered to me that he thought it was a bad joke and that I took it very well. I merely smiled. That Shekhar always sidles up to me whenever he gets a chance; I find his clumsy advances rather amusing. He is harmless, really, though annoying at times; but then, most men appear harmless when you've reached that premenopausal age. It is different with women, though. Especially the younger ones. They can be more than merely annoying with their pert bodies and empty minds; like Juhi, for instance.

Juhi is always in need of recipes, especially on Sunday mornings when I am busy in the kitchen and Hem is tinkering with his model planes and ships in the veranda. So, invariably, he is the first person she meets as she sways her hips up to our door. Hem, seated on a cane chair, is concentrating on a bent wing or propeller, his elbows on the glass-topped white cane table, beads of perspiration glistening on his nose. Juhi slides up to him and takes out her white handkerchief at the same time. So far, she has not had the gumption to wipe the sweat off Hem's face. But she always stands there, hoping, I suppose, for Hem to invite her. Hem continues fiddling with his models. She looks at him suggestively, and says, 'Hi Hem! Playing with your toys again?'

Hem obliges by giving her his baby bright smile and says, 'Yeah. You want to join me?'

Juhi promptly starts to giggle, albeit a tad nervously. If Ravi is around, he spoils her fun by saying, 'Aunty, look! This one is dad's latest,' before commencing on a long explanation about the intricacies of that particular model. It is the 'aunty' bit that always spoils her mood, I know.

My daughter, Riya, is more direct, but she leaves out the aunty, part. 'Oh, hello there,' she says, giving Juhi a swift and casual, but irksome nonetheless, once-over, 'Ma's in the kitchen in case you want a recipe.' After that, Juhi has no choice but to come to the kitchen where I am supervising the cook. Hem, of course, continues as if nothing has happened.

Sometimes I wonder whether he acts innocent on purpose. Just to avoid a discussion with me. His twinkling eyes can easily be misunderstood. Surely, he knows that it *is* flirtatious to grin so disarmingly at a woman who is obviously acting coy? How can he not be aware of himself, of me, and us and them, all those women?! How can he be so oblivious of the men's sneaky advances? Especially when all of them are his office colleagues and friends he's known for donkey's years? Usually, I try not to think like this; thoughts such like these are bad for my skin. That is why when they do invade my head, I take a nap with two slices of chilled cucumber slices on my eyelids. But when you've been married for as many years as we have, you should not take small things too lightly. A balance must always be maintained. A stitch in time saves nine, I always say. A timely precaution can save a marriage, no matter how petty the issue may appear.

Riya had been whining about a ten-day photography camp in her college. We finally relented and allowed her to go, even though the prospect of her staying out for more than a week made me feel uncomfortable. She is a young, impressionable girl after all. But Hem was okay with it. So, she went to the camp, and returned after ten days with a friend in tow.

'Ma,' she said blithely. 'This is Anu; she'd like to stay with us for a few days. You don't mind, I hope?'

'No, of course not,' said Hem, before I could speak, smiling at Anu. 'Hello, Anu.'

I disliked Anu from the very first day. She was a simpering little thing who had let her black hair grow long, like Rapunzel's, and she had eyes so wide and guileless that you would think she could be trusted with your worst secret. To make matters worse, that slip of a girl was a know-it-all! She knew almost as much about the kitchen as my cook did—I doubt she knew as much as I, but she did try—except that I was smarter and hid all my recipe books. It seemed as if she had done some homework on model planes, for she appeared to be quite adept at identifying the various parts, much to Ravi's and Hem's delight. She knew a thing or two about dressing up too, and dress up she did, both herself and Riya, until I had a hard time recognizing my own baby. Within two days of her arrival, she had taken over our lives completely, participating in everything that each of us said or did. Everybody loved her; even Hem, who normally does not notice any of Riya's friends, took to her quite nicely.

Anu's stay with us kept getting extended, until we reached the middle of the month. Nobody in the family seemed to want her to leave, except for me. The cook, who normally starts grumbling one day after a guest extends his or her stay, hummed as he worked on that second bowl of curry or plate of halva. The gardener arrived dutifully every morning with flowers for the vases that I had placed all over the house, even though they have strict instructions to wait for two days before replenishing the vases. 'Anu Didi was admiring the lilies, memsaab,' he said, handing over a bunch of half-blossomed lilies I was saving for the kitty party on Saturday. Even Ravi spent hours trailing Anu up and down the garden until she relented and played carom with him or took him along when she and Riya went swimming at the club.

Things got worse as the days passed and they became more and more familiar with each other. Hem started coming home earlier to take the children to the club or the lake. 'After all it's their summer vacation, Tara.'

As if I didn't know the real reason. I am not suspicious of Hem; it's just that I am justifiably wary of scheming females. Hem is after all a man, a good one at that, a caring father, a responsible husband, and funny too. But he won't hesitate before sowing his wild oats if he gets the opportunity, I know. Which man would? It is up to the woman to keep her home clean and germ-free, I always say.

Of course, I went along with them wherever they went. Outwardly, I was a picture of grace and dignity, despite the sly remarks of some of our acquaintances whom we met during these outings. 'This is exactly what I would look for in a bride for my son,' one matriarch said. 'Oh, look at them, they are like sisters,' another cooed. But Shekhar was the worst, 'Wow, Tara,' he whispered, 'you look so lovely tonight. You can put any young thing to shame.' He gave me the slyest of looks to see how I had taken his jibe. I have nerves of steel. I never let on anything to anyone. I just counted the days, waiting for the vacation to get over, and that wretched girl to go back to wherever she came from. I was not going to make a scene at any cost, even though I wanted to box her ears every time I caught her laughing with Hem.

Anu shared Riya's room, which is downstairs. Ravi's room is right next to Riya's. They share a common bathroom which opens out into the corridor leading to the hall. There is another small but well-furbished bathroom under the stairs, but this one is exclusively for guests, though Hem and

I use it whenever it feels like too much effort to run upstairs. Actually, there are no strict rules as to who will use which bathroom. However, when guests come, especially relatives from Hem's side, I keep my bathroom out of bounds. By the end of the first week of Anu's stay, she had already made one or two forays into my sanctum sanctorum—that was because she had wormed her way in so well that she was almost part of the family; she told me so herself.

'Oh, aunty, you are so sweet. I already feel like I'm part of your family. Now, how did you say you wanted the potatoes cut?'

I hadn't said anything about the potatoes. The cook was supposed to do the potatoes, and he instantly materialized, with a betel-nut-stained grin plastered on his face. I just walked out of the kitchen and went into the garden. The gardener was there, fiddling with some tools. I scowled in reply to his 'salaam memsaab'. I thought I'd sit on the swing for a while. I have to pass Riya's bedroom to get to the swing. This part where their bathroom window opens is a little secluded from the rest of the garden. A fully-grown bougainvillea, spread out between two poles, acts like a screen to maintain the privacy of the rooms. Previously, the dog used to be stationed here during the day, but now Jimmy is dead and nobody comes here any more. On an impulse, I decided to pop into this secluded place. I saw a ladder propped up against the bathroom wall. That was odd. I called the gardener and asked him who had put it there.

'I don't know, memsaab. Saab was asking for the ladder three days ago.' His answer irritated me, and I curtly told him to take the ladder away. I returned to the house. I was suddenly in no mood to sit on the swing.

The day continued as usual without any incident. There was a whist drive at the club that evening. I was keen to go so I suggested we all have dinner at the club. I was ready by six o' clock, and so were my children and Hem. Our guest, however, needed more time. Ravi, Riya and I waited for her in the hall while Hem went off to potter around his car. Suddenly, there was a shriek. All of us rushed to Riya's bedroom. Anu was there, wearing a housecoat and little else, and pointing towards the bathroom and shaking.

'The man! The man! The man!' was all she could say in her hysteria.

After some time, when we had spent more than our quota of energy soothing her and making her drink some water, we managed to get her to be sufficiently calm enough to tell us what had happened. From what she babbled, it looked like someone had tried to enter her bedroom through the bathroom (possibly the skylight in the bathroom, because the window had a cast-iron grille fixed to it) when she was about to shed her housecoat for something more appropriate. The man was tallish, that was all she could make out. He was in the shadows, so she hadn't been able to see his face. He fled when she screamed. We went out to check. The ladder was still there, but now it was lying on its side. Anu and Riya immediately wanted to change bedrooms with Hem and me. I promised to sleep in the next bedroom and shift Ravi upstairs. Nobody was in the mood to go anywhere after all the hullabaloo. I would have to miss my whist drive at the club, but for once, I didn't mind. I had some bidding to do at home, and who knew, if I played my cards right, my evening could be salvaged after all! I looked forward to that.

Hem was nowhere in sight all this time. And when he finally came in, he looked hot and wanted to change his shirt again. I followed him into our bedroom. 'Someone tried to get into the girls' bedroom today,' I said. Hem looked at me startled. 'Why?' he said. I wanted to hit him—what a question!

'Hem, I said someone tried to get to Anu in the bedroom this evening. That person must have got in through the bathroom skylight. I can't think of any other possibility. By the way, the gardener told me that you took the ladder a couple of days ago,' I looked at Hem directly as I spoke.

Hem shifted uneasily, 'Looks like you're accusing me of something. God! Tara, she's just a kid. And a weird one at that.'

Now I was really suspicious. 'Weird? Why do you say that? I thought you liked her well enough.'

Hem turned around to look at me. 'Tara, she strikes funny poses in the bathroom with a black stole wrapped around her in this heat, staring at herself in the mirror.' Then seeing my horrified face, he gulped. 'Look, Tara, I was only looking for that stupid golf ball I lost while practising in the garden. Those damn balls keep flying off . . . Tara! You know me better than that!'

'Hem! How could you peek into her bathroom? Couldn't you come inside the house and look for the golf ball? You're pathetic. What if she had seen you?'

'The ball fell on the window shed, Tara! Why should I look for it inside? Besides, it was only for a split second. I didn't know there was anyone in the bathroom. And why was her window wide open, eh? Oh! I wish you wouldn't insist I play that stupid game.' With that, Hem stomped off to the bathroom in a huff, with a 'be glad I didn't smash the panes'!

I was sure Anu had seen Hem. That was why she insisted that whoever had entered her room was tall. Hem, of course, deserved to be drowned in a pickle vat for being so stupid. I hoped, though I did not entirely believe it, that he had learnt his lesson. Cursing Hem under my breath, I went downstairs and had a quiet word with Anu. After that unpleasant task, I went out into the garden and had another not very quiet word with the gardener. I gave him his wages with a strict warning that just a phone call from me could land him in jail. Afterwards, I insisted that we all go to the club and have dinner, even though we had all but missed the whist drive.

Anu cut short her stay and went home. Riya, to my delight, actually looked relieved. Ravi was delighted that we were going to keep a dog again, especially since I promised to let the mutt sleep in the house, in his bedroom. The dog would come after I had all the bathroom skylights permanently sealed. I decided that we could no longer compromise on the safety of our home for the sake of aesthetics. Actually, I was grateful to Anu for inadvertently throwing light on a potential weak point in my otherwise fortress-like home.

I cornered Hem soon after Anu's departure, 'Now are you going to tell me the truth or not, Hem?' I looked at him square in the eye. 'How good is your eyesight?'

Hem grinned sheepishly.

'No more playing the fool, Hem! We are going to the ophthalmologist tomorrow, okay?'

Hem made a wry face. 'I hate specs. Makes one look like a nerdy prof. *You* look like a school matron, you know that?' he said, watching me closely for the effect of his words. I shrugged it off, so he tried again. 'Yeah, you look just like one of those crabby old biddies forever spying on girls young enough to be their sons' girlfriends!'

Hem looked satisfied with his salvo and began casually flipping the pages of a magazine. He even twiddled his toes.

'Hem, had you been wearing specs that day, you would have seen Anu with her Rapunzel hair wrapped around her. That's what she wanted, that little cuckoo!'

Hem stopped flipping the pages. 'Now she tells me!' he said, rolling his eyes.

'Hem,' I said. 'Quit clowning. Have you even a clue about what goes on? Sometimes right under your nose?' Hem looked innocently at the wall. 'Hem,' I said again. 'Are you aware that your dear pal Shekhar never leaves a chance to flirt with me?'

Hem, still looking innocent, headed for the door. 'Keep him dangling till he gets me that new model plane he promised on his next trip abroad,' he said and slipped out of the room before my pillow could find its mark.

SEXLESS IN SINGAPORE

The first thing that Naina noticed when she passed through the customs at Changi Airport was how easily, and even nonchalantly, the women carried themselves in their skimpy clothes. She immediately felt fat and dowdy in her salwar-kameez. She wished she'd worn her Levis.

Naina had grown up in an environment where swimsuits and tennis shorts, and dresses for Saturday-night dancing were normal. But Naina's mother wouldn't dream of letting her daughter go shopping in shorts and other 'revealing' clothes. Group dates were all right as long as your parents knew the boys' parents and vice versa, and everybody knew where you were going and what you would be doing. But these restrictions did not necessarily apply to her brothers and their friends. So Naina learnt early that girls were girls and boys were boys, and the twain could never truly meet on equal ground. Not in India, at least.

Naina was twenty-three years old when she married her engineering college batchmate and sweetheart Nilesh (Neil to Naina and their friends). Now two years after playing the nice traditional daughter-in-law, Naina was relieved to see that they were in a place where she hoped she could be more herself. Her old self, the one that Neil had fallen for. Except that she wasn't sure whether Neil really cared to have the old Naina back.

'Sometimes I feel like a bloody doll!' she had grumbled to Neil once, out of the earshot of their large retinue of in-laws.

Neil had given her his lopsided grin and said, 'Yeah! One that's owned by me!'

It was no use talking to Neil about how she felt. If she started a serious discussion, he reminded her that she came from a privileged background and had no business talking about deprivation and all that.

'I mean, look at you,' he said. 'You have the best of both worlds! You have money and education and you are an Indian woman. You don't *have* to work; you don't have any social and economic pressures to bring home the bacon. And you are hardly expected to break your back doing housework. You have independence, but few responsibilities. Seriously Nin, forget about the poor and underprivileged women in our own country, women in the West would give their right arms to be in your shoes!'

Neil didn't understand. And she couldn't explain to him either, her need to be her own true self without being a woman first. The thought itself, when she strung it out in her own mind, seemed complicated. She felt feminine enough, but she did not want everything to be about her sex. She needed sexual invisibility to some extent. All this was quite challenging; she could feel it, but could barely articulate it even to herself. The strappy top and shorts had nothing specific to do with her need. The outfit was just a way of expressing herself. She could swing a bare leg and shrug a nude shoulder without incurring the winks and crude remarks of street Romeos. She could be herself, another attractive human being, without bothering about the cause and effect of what she wore. Naina decided she would.

The first few months were spent trawling the malls, just looking; maybe picking up a tank top here and a pair of cropped pants there. Neil had started wearing shorts everywhere, except to work, much sooner than she did, like everybody else in Singapore. 'Shorts are the national dress here' was the standard declaration they heard from expats and locals alike. Perhaps that was why he didn't bat an eyelid when she stood before him in a pair of itsy-bitsy denim shorts, for the first time since their marriage. Naina was slightly irked. But she said nothing. Instead, she went on a wardrobe-overhauling binge with a vengeance.

Armed with information gleaned from *Her World*, *CittaBella* and sundry fashion magazines, one eye peeled wide to catch the latest trends, Naina shopped, till Neil literally dropped from his chair as he totted up his credit card bills one day.

'So, you noticed I'm wearing different clothes? Finally!' she accused him.

'Did you give me a choice?'

'Nice to know that money talks, even though I'm invisible!'

'But I thought that is exactly what you wanted to be!' he countered. 'Remember how dowdy you felt in your salwar–kameez, when we first came here? You wanted to merge with the crowd. Well, you have! I have the bill to prove it!'

Naina shrugged. She did not want to let this minor cloud discourage her. Especially now that she was out to trim herself literally down to size. Neil was happily ignorant of her plans.

Naina was considered slim in India. But here, in Singapore, where a twenty-eight-inch waist was considered broad, her slim Indian figure seemed extra-large in comparison. Everywhere Naina looked, she saw sylph-like apparitions. She was convinced that the road to being her own true self was clogged by fatty tissue. Naina looked at herself critically in the bathroom mirror as she pondered. If she didn't diet, but went jogging in the morning, how much would she lose? Perhaps she should do the Cambridge diet. She could also join a weight-loss centre, though the gym downstairs seemed a cheaper option. Naina decided to pop a few diet pills for starters.

Slimming tea was next on the agenda, along with jogs in the park. But it didn't seem to work for her. Their weekend binges at Clarke Quay, Quay pubs and the East Coast Road eateries were, Naina suspected, the real culprits behind her muffin top and heavy thighs. But giving up these weekend treats that she washed down with beer or wine would be too much of a sacrifice. Both she and Neil looked forward to the weekends. That was when they met up with their few but steadily growing circle of friends. Besides, what else was there to do in Singapore? You could go to the zoo and the bird park and Sentosa for just so many times; hanging out at the malls with Neil was no fun—he was a shop-only-when-necessary kind of guy and hated window shopping. Slipping away every weekend to next-door Malaysia was too expensive, even if you took the train instead of driving down. They both needed these weekends with their friends.

Naina made up her mind to lose the extra weight despite the weekends. It would also give her something to do apart from doing the rounds with her resume. That was another bane, and a humiliating one at that, especially when she was well-qualified.

'I need to look more like a local,' she muttered to herself. 'Really blend in with the crowd.'

It was no longer a matter of just becoming invisible sex-wise. She had to feel completely at ease with her surroundings. Naina hit the gym in the mornings and the park's jogging track in the evenings. She started eating salads without dressing, and drinking coffee without sugar and cream. She drank less beer and more water during the weekend binges. And she popped a Xenical or two in the privacy of the bathroom every time they ate Indian food or went to an Indian friend's house party.

While Neil got busy with his work and began coming home later than usual, Naina became more familiar with the fellow joggers in the park—some of them were even on smiling terms with her! Naina went to the gym reasonably late in the morning, not early, for that was when the office-goers and students dropped in for a quick run on the treadmills. She went right after the office crowd, but before the housewives trooped in. Naina did not feel like a housewife. She felt ashamed to associate with women who talked about cooking and babies. She had been a working woman until just before they arrived in Singapore. She had yet to get used to responding to the apparently harmless query 'So, what do you do?' with 'I am a housewife' or the more politically correct 'I am a homemaker' sort of reply. Naina usually deflected the question with a shrug, a smile, and a, 'Oh, I'm just weighing my options right now. Enjoying the break, you know!'

The truth couldn't be further off the mark. Naina had been doing the rounds with her portfolio and posting her resume on job portals diligently, but with little success. The slice of anger wedged in her heart seemed to grow fatter with every returned or ignored resume. And that fat went straight to her belly and thighs. She began to act more and more intellectually superior to the locals, as well as the plump Indian women so engrossed in their husbands, their brats, their small worlds. She started to swim longer laps in their condo's pool.

Neil joined her during the weekends when they did not have a party to attend. He swam lazily and sometimes floated on his back gazing up at the stars with a dreamy look on his face. Naina noticed how soft Neil looked beside the hard and wiry Singaporean men. Neil was tall and broad-shouldered, but a fondness for beer and what he termed 'good food' gave him a roundness that had lately begun to irritate Naina.

One day, feeling particularly good-humoured, Neil sang while he floated, 'I am sailing . . . I am sailing . . . I am sailing, across the seas . . .'

He sounded out of tune and Naina gave him a quick glance of irritation. But most of the people there at the pool, including some pretty, young and achingly slim Singaporean ladies laughed delightedly. Neil had his lopsided grin aimed at the ladies which they acknowledged with a wave. Having noticed that, Naina continued doing a backstroke with swift vengeful strikes.

'You're becoming quite a hit with the ladies here,' she said when they were both in bed, but not snuggling. 'I thought you didn't care for flat chests!'

Neil turned towards her with a look that showed both surprise and contempt, 'What's wrong with you? Did you realize you sound like a rebuffed bitch?'

'You're calling me a bitch? Is that what you say to your own wife?'

'I didn't call you a bitch; I said you sounded like one.'

'It's the same thing!'

'It is not! Besides, Nin, you should see and hear yourself nowadays. You've got your claws out at everyone. What's eating you? As it is, you look like a bag of bones . . .'

'Shut up! Just shut up! You're the one who's bitching now!'

Neil shut up and turned to the other side while Naina sobbed as silently as she could.

The next morning, Neil got up early again and sneaked off to get a McDonald's breakfast for them. He saw her swollen eyes looking at this rare treat (rare because she had been completely avoiding McDonald's and similar fast food) with pleasure, and his heart wrenched with love and pity for her. He bunked office that day and followed her around like a puppy, until she relented. He pushed her down on the bed. But they both sensed something was missing.

Not wanting to spoil the mood, Naina suggested they go for a movie. Neil was grateful for the suggestion, because, suddenly, the day had started to loom large before him, filling him up with a sense of helplessness.

Neil woke up earlier the next day and got ready in a hurry. He wanted to make up for his absence by reaching office before everybody else.

'Aren't you going to finish your coffee?' said Naina as she scrutinized the *Straits Times*. Neil took another sip and fled. Now Naina stared at the white walls, her mind not moving, her eyes not blinking.

A mynah sat on a window sill and cocked its cheeky head at her. Naina made a pretence of throwing something at it. The bird did not budge, but twitched its tail at her, squawking rudely. Naina turned away to clear the dishes. The part-time help was due any moment, so she just piled them in the sink and wiped the table. She and Neil had decided against keeping a full-time Indonesian maid for the time being. Instead, they had a part-time Sri Lankan maid, who came in three times a week to clean the house and iron the clothes. She charged ten dollars an hour, a fortune compared to what they would have been paying back home. But her work was far superior to any maid even her mother had experienced in India. The vessels didn't remain oily after she washed them, there was no dust or grime on the floors or furniture surfaces, and the bathrooms sparkled. Naina's cousin, who had followed her husband to the US, regularly complained about the lack of help and barely any public transport. Secretly, Naina was glad to be in Singapore, which gave her the best of both worlds. She was glad she didn't have to do the drudgery in the house, at least most of it. That would have demeaned her beyond redemption. But she didn't say that to Neil, who considered moving to the US a promotion over his colleagues in Singapore and India.

Naina gave the gym a miss that day. In the evening, she went to the park, hoping to fill the emptiness inside her. She did not jog. She strolled around, trying not to catch the eyes of the regulars. After a while, Naina found an empty seat near the children's play area and sat down. She wished she had a book with her, at least she could have pretended to read instead of announcing her emptiness to anyone who cared to notice.

Nobody looked at her. A young Chinese–Singaporean mother was busy encouraging her four-year-old daughter to try the slide, while she juggled a six-month-old baby in her arms. An old Malay-Singaporean couple chattered softly amongst themselves, while keeping an eye on their grandchildren—two round boys and a plump girl gambolling around. A man, who looked neither Chinese nor Malay nor Tamil, but a bit of all three, played 'choo-choo' train with his four children. A pair of Indian ladies, who didn't look local, and were probably expatriates like Naina, sat gossiping on the bench while their babies sat in their prams. Their bench was close enough for the conversation to reach Naina's ears.

Some words caught Naina's attention as she fiddled with her cell phone. The Indian women were discussing the

Singaporean woman sitting nearby. They were speaking in Hindi. But Naina could tell by the way her jaw tightened that the woman understood she was being discussed, even as she continued to attend to her children.

Naina pretended to make a call as she eavesdropped. The women spoke in such audible whispers that Naina wondered why they were bothering to keep up the pretence at all.

'My God, these people are so small,' tittered one, in a mix of Hindi and broken English.

'I know ya. I can't find bras for my size here. Mine are like bazookas, you know,' replied the other.

'Oh! That's so funny!' the other woman chuckled. 'It's the same with me, y'know! My God! They are so flat ya! You can't even make out which one's a girl, which one's boy!'

'So un-feminine, no?'

'I know ya! Look at that one with two children also!'

'But nothing to show. No?'

The two women chattered on, gloating over their buxomness, their words riding like gadflies in the breeze. After some time, their conversation drifted on to other meatier topics, mostly gossip about other members of their own social circle. Naina watched the women covertly. Compared with the delicately boned Singaporean woman, these two appeared ungainly and were too broad, like a pair of bolsters with arms and legs. Their babies with kohl-smeared eyes looked small and underfed by contrast. The women were sitting cross-kneed and Naina could see their shabby sandals dangling below their cracked and dirty feet adorned with silver anklets and toe rings. Their ears and noses sparkled with diamonds, and thick gold bangles clinked on their wrists. Naina grimaced slightly as she looked away. The two Indian women were more alien to her than the Singaporean lady they had been gossiping about moments ago. She would never have met them in India. Their worlds were oceans apart.

After a while, as if in a single choreographed movement, the three mothers started to feed their babies, except for one small difference. The two Indian women produced milk bottles which they thrust in their babies' mouths without stopping their conversation. The Singaporean mother deftly put her baby's head inside her T-shirt, and in a single fluid movement, threw a light shawl over her shoulder. She held the infant close under the shawl, while she suckled.

Naina watched the little pantomime for a few minutes; what the two women did would have seemed perfectly ordinary to Naina had the Singaporean woman not been present. To Naina's freshly turned eyes, the nursing mother looked more natural and decent than they.

Naina put her phone down. Something buzzed inside her head. She swallowed and leaned towards the breast-feeding young woman.

'Hi! Um, I, well I hope you don't mind, but you seem to be managing two so easily . . . Isn't it difficult? You know, sometimes, I feel so scared; don't know how I'll manage with one . . .' said Naina, laughing awkwardly.

The woman looked up, momentarily startled. Then she smiled.

'Don't feel scared, la. It's simple, really simple. You know, after a while you get used to it . . .'

'Tell me how you do it? Tell me how you are so happy doing it?' her heart seemed to say. Instead, Naina smiled and leaned closer, 'Babies are so delicate. Like porcelain dolls.'

The woman laughed. 'Yes, yes, like doll. But no need to be scared. It's natural.'

She pulled down her T-shirt and expertly burped her baby. Turning towards Naina, she confided that she had been afraid too when it was her first time. As she listened, Naina found herself getting more and more drawn into the woman's world, and her experiences of motherhood. Naina leaned forward to hold the baby's fingers. The infant gurgled and smiled. A different sensation swept through Naina's veins from the tips of her fingers where her skin met the baby's.

When Naina returned home, she felt her body was at ease with itself, after what seemed like a whole age. A quiet joy wrapped softly around her, like a Pashmina stole. It shut out the cacophony of her life, the residue of the two women's mindless meanness. Neil hadn't returned from work yet. Dusk flowed in through the open windows. The distant sloshing of waves from the sea was restful to her ears. It occurred to Naina then that the sounds of the sea had always been there, an auditory embrace. But she hadn't noticed it before.

MISSING THE MOVIE

'There is no life here, brother!' Sanat chewed his paan, before expertly squirting the red juice on the road at a neat forty-five-degree angle. '*Saala*, India is shining, but we are still burning. Why, my brothers, I am asking you, why? Our country is shining because rich Indians are diamonds? Brothers, we are also diamonds. So why are *we* burning?' He looked at his friends bitterly and continued without waiting for any of them to reply. 'Because we are the black diamonds, brothers. We are the coals. Coal is black diamond, no? We are the fuel of India. If we don't burn, how will India shine?'

This speech invariably brought on nods and murmurs of agreement and encouraged political commentary from the gang. But Girish kept quiet, even though he secretly agreed with Sanat that Dubki-Talliya had no life. For Girish was, after all, the pampered younger son, who had passed his school's final examination and acquired a wife who had studied up to Class XII, unlike most of his friends and Bade Bhaisaab—his elder brother, who was a simple, thumb-signature peasant, and Bhabiji, Bade Bhaisaab's equally illiterate wife.

Girish pitied his brother and sister-in-law. How basic and boring their existence was. The thought irritated him. They were like a pair of buffaloes, content to chew cud and get kicked around by life's circumstances. If it wasn't for their continued presence, which was as good as interference, Girish would have sold the land and taken his wife and mother to Delhi to try his luck a long time ago.

Sanat, at least, had tried. His bitterness and dissatisfaction with life at Dubki-Talliya, a barely visible-on-the-map town on the border of Bihar and Uttar Pradesh, was well known. Sanat was Delhi-returned and his ruminations on life in the capital, which were endless and wistful at the start, grew more and more desperate as the days went by and his chances of returning to Delhi diminished. For Pandit Maharaj, the town vaid, had given Sanat an ultimatum—his leg would not get better, but if they were lucky, it could be kept from getting worse. Since Dubki-Talliya's most respected vaid was all Sanat and his family could afford, this ultimatum was the end of the road. Well, almost. For Sanat was a dreamer. And these days, he spun his dreams around the tales he told his cronies.

Girish and his friends liked listening to Sanat's stories, especially the ones that were hardest to believe. They crowded around Sanat after their work at the kiln got over. They gathered at Hanumanji's peepul tree, where Sanat recited his Delhi anecdotes like a mantra, and Girish and the rest listened, laughed, nodded and egged him on, while the red stone statue of Hanumanji grinned from the gnarled trunks of the ancient peepul. Perhaps Sanat understood their need to listen to something fantastic and bold, not unlike the heroics displayed in Hindi movies. Girish and his friends, on their part, empathized with Sanat's need to amuse and instruct as much as they enjoyed his stories.

Sanat told them about life in Delhi, which was a whole new world away from Dubki-Talliya. Delhi was where all the airplanes of the world—especially the jets that left chalky white lines on the sky—swooped down. It was the city where smartly dressed young people sat in front of computers with attached phones and talked to people at the other end of the world in the wonderful English language spoken by the movie stars of the English films that were shown once a month in Dubki-Talliya's solitary cinema hall. Delhi was where silently cruising *phoren* cars never belched smoke, and shimmering shopping malls spilled over with unimaginable luxuries and sparkling buildings as tall as mountains stood. Sanat told them about houses that were made entirely of glass. He spoke rapturously of frothy fountains inside apartments, fifteen storeys above ground. He told them about malls that were as big as towns and even housed air-conditioned cinema houses that could run six movies at the same time in different halls, and the bejewelled people who ate and drank at glittering restaurants.

Sanat didn't speak much about himself and the life that he had during those few years in Delhi. He didn't tell them about the precarious ladders he had to climb in order to clean the glass fronts of tall buildings and the private welding and cleaning jobs that he had done on Sundays and other public holidays, just to earn the extra cash he sent by money order to his mother. He never referred to the limp in his left leg. His friends never learnt how lucky he considered himself just to be alive. After that fateful day when he fell on his colleague's broken body during a window cleaning session, because the rotted coconut fibre chord around his waist and the other around his unlucky co-worker's waist had unravelled suddenly, causing the two men to plummet down two floors. Sanat had sustained an injury that had left him permanently lame and unfit for further work in Delhi. He had been given five thousand rupees as compensation because some of the men in their group knew someone who was on good terms with a union leader somewhere with political connections. And, Sanat had returned to Dubki-Talliya, unfit for any labour that a rural life demanded, but full of stories and his

Delhi-returned swagger, albeit with a limp. Girish and his cronies never laughed at Sanat. Lame or not, he was a heroic figure. And his stories filled them with hopes and dreams.

Girish lived with his wife Seema, widowed mother, Bade Bhaisaab, Bhabiji, and their two boys in a lime-washed house, among a row of similar houses in a dusty lane, scattered with dogs, goats, cows and their pats, the tring-tring of bicycles and the shouts of dirty half-naked children. Everything was as shabby as the other lanes criss-crossing Dubki-Talliya.

Girish's life was an unending row of identical days. Hanging out with Sanat and going to the occasional cinema were virtually the only modes of entertainment available, unless you counted watching serials on their second-hand TV, which, though enjoyable, was not an outing, because one could only watch the Doordarshan broadcast programmes. Cable connections, dish antennae and all those exotic gadgets Sanat spoke about were beyond their reach. Due to lack of entertainment, Girish's dreams took on the cellophane colours of Hindi movies. His yearnings, stretching further north towards the smooth pukka roads of Delhi, needed the larger-than-life celluloid heroes and heroines to provide succour to his glamour- and excitement-starved soul.

Girish wished Seema could also hang out with him and his friends. He wished he could buy skirts and dresses for her to wear. And shiny high-heeled shoes. But Seema could not 'hang out', since she was the daughter-in-law, and cinema was too expensive an option to make it a regular outing. Seema felt as left out as Girish wanted her in. That was not good for Girish's marital happiness. So, Girish saved from his salary, and promised Seema that they would not just go to the cinema, but they would go to watch an English film and have Coca-Cola afterwards. She had never seen an English film in her life. It would be a treat she would never forget.

Dubki-Talliya's cinema hall was located in the main bazaar, where it attracted a motley crowd of loiterers, who often came in just to escape the blazing sun. The cinema hall was housed in a brick building with an asbestos roof. An old neem tree extended its gnarled boughs over the roof, which was pockmarked by last year's hail. Hairline cracks on the roof allowed streaks of sunlight to pour into the hall below. The loiterers were not unwelcome, and old Mahadeo Pandey, the security guard-cum-usher-cum-ticket-checker, never shooed them away. They provided company when the shows were on, and tea and gossip during other times.

Nobody bought the tickets in advance. Those who were rich or desperate enough bought their tickets in black. Most men dressed up in fine clothes and swaggered up to the queue. Tickets for *angrezi* movies were rarely sold by the ticket-blackers, unless they had explicit scenes and lots of bare flesh. In that case the news would travel fast and far and every pipsqueak worth the pip in his pants would line up and the ticket-blackers would have a field day. These days, the Hindi films were no different, but old ideas die hard and the once-a-month English movie continued to be screened successfully.

Girish and the others of his ilk never bought tickets from the blackers, even for the greatest Hindi films. It was too expensive; he preferred to take his chances at the ticket counter. He usually joined the queue and prayed to Hanumanji of the peepul tree to ensure the tickets lasted till at least his turn was over. The really lucky ones were those who went with their womenfolk, because the ladies had a separate queue, which was considerably shorter. Many louts would request the ladies, 'Behenji or Bhabiji or Maji (depending on the perceived age or status of the woman), please get me one ticket, only one, no, make it two, please, we are standing for one hour and I have weak heart.' This would prompt some of the ladies to jeer: 'Will your weak heart withstand all the fighting scenes in the cinema?' Titters and laughter would follow. But if the fellow was persistent, one kind soul would buy his ticket for him.

Getting the tickets, however, was not Girish's problem today. He hummed a tune as he applied attar on his moustache and glanced at Seema. Seema's face was covered with her ghungat, so he did not catch the expression on her face. Although she was a modern girl and did not keep her face covered when she went out with him alone, out of respect for the elders she followed the rules at home. Girish liked that, modern but not too modern, though he would often whisper his fantasy of seeing her in a *mem*-style dress in the privacy of their room, and she would giggle shyly as she traced the hair growing in a straight line upto his naval.

They left shortly afterwards. Girish was sitting upright on the scooter, his open-button kurta showing off the silver chain and pendant resting on his chest, while Seema was seated behind him, a striking picture in her peacock bright nylon sari, with a coy hand on her husband's shoulder. If she was aware of the sneaky stares that followed them, her posture did not betray it. They arrived a good half hour before the show. Girish counted the notes and handed them to Seema. She smiled as she took them, her head uncovered for the entire world to admire her kohled eyes, the dimple on her left cheek and the sidelocks that she had oiled and curled into stiff upside-down question marks lying pat against her cheeks. Seema was a wise girl; she kept up to date on the gossip and latest trends, but she also kept her mother-in-law happy. Girish's mother was all praises for her younger *bahurani*, her favourite son's bride. The other reason for her good opinion, of course, rested on the fact that Seema's father had provided not one but two scooters as dowry, one for Girish and one for his elder brother.

'We didn't even ask,' Girish's mother had gushed later. 'I only said in passing that neither of my sons rode scooters, and it's so hot travelling by bus all the time.' She had looked around her to observe the effects of this statement, and her listeners dutifully nodded their heads in approval, their tobacco-stuffed mouths moving in rhythm. What the elder daughter-in-law thought about this generosity, nobody knew, for she was a silent woman, as silent as her stolid farmer husband. But she and Seema seemed to share a good relationship. Seema never overlooked her status as the elder bahurani and the mother of Chunnu and Munnu, the only heirs of their family. Girish was modern (too modern according to his fond but worried mother and some elderly relatives who loudly disapproved) and took the precautions extolled by the government. He had decided that he and Seema would have at least three years of bliss before they went for the government-endorsed '*chhota pariwar, sukhi pariwar*' policy of one and only one child.

Seema, being the ever-tactful sister-in-law, had earlier invited the elder one for the movie, whom she called 'Didi' to join her, but the latter had declined graciously, much to Seema's relief. They wouldn't have been able to watch the movie freely, and besides what would Didi possibly do at the screening of an English movie? With duty out of the way, Seema had hurried away to wear her bright red plastic bangles and matching slippers.

Girish looked around the cinema hall to see if there were any familiar faces. He saw Sanat and exchanged cursory greetings. Sanat gave Seema the eye, but discreetly. There were other familiar faces, friends of his elder brother and Bhabiji. One or two had even brought their wives and children along. Entry for children up to the age of twelve years were free. So many parents fiercely crusaded for their children's rights to remain children and enjoy the reduced price for a cinema ticket for an improbably long time, but Mahadeo Pandey knew better than to argue with an aggressive mother.

Girish and Seema slipped past Mahadeo Pandey who grinned at everyone as if he knew their worst secrets. Girish had his hand possessively placed around Seema's waist. Seated in the dim-lit hall, Girish stretched his arm around Seema's shoulder. Seema squirmed a little, giggled softly, and then settled down to enjoy this public display of romance. One of the female patrons commented not too softly on how forward some couples had become these days. A wag from the semi-darkness beyond advised the lady to get her own husband to follow suit. Titters followed, but were soon drowned by the advertisements that were shown before the actual movie began.

Girish and Seema watched the advertisements intently; they devoured the fabulous settings as well as the antics and postures of the models that endorsed the products. The cinema-hall owner made sure there was a long series of advertisements preceding the actual movie, especially on English-movie days, since these films were much shorter than the Hindi film sagas. The advertisements ended and the interval began. This was the cue for all the vendors to enter and start plying their wares. Peanut vendors, bhelpuri-wallahs, ice-cream vendors, masala chai-wallahs, candyfloss vendors with their shocking pink clouds of spun sugar trooped into the hall.

Girish stretched his legs and beckoned the man selling cooldrinks. The man acknowledged him, and then motioned him to wait as he turned to attend to a customer who was closer. Girish was annoyed. He stood up to see who had usurped his vendor, and gaped. Seated four rows ahead of him were Bade Bhaisaab and Bhabiji, with neither Chunnu nor Munnu in sight. The vendor was handing two freshly opened bottles of *thanda* Cola to Bade Bhaisaab. Girish sat down and nudged Seema. She craned her neck to see and immediately collapsed into her seat, giggling.

'Arrey ji,' said Seema to her bemused husband. 'What are Didi and Bade Bhaisaab doing here?' Girish shook his head. He was too shocked to answer.

The man selling the cooldrinks came over, but Girish waved him away. Seema pouted, but Girish was too distracted to notice. Seema didn't say anything, but inwardly seethed at the slyness Didi had displayed. Bade Bhaisaab may be the elder brother but he did not earn as much as Girish. The difference in their status was obvious every time Maji returned from the temple and rested her auspicious flame-warmed hand on Seema's head first, even before she blessed her beloved Chunnu and Munnu. Didi was becoming competitive, Seema told herself. But she was also puzzled. They had never come to see a movie together by themselves. Didi and Bade Bhaisaab never went anywhere without the entire family—Maji, Chunnu-Munnu and even Seema and Girish—in tow. She had only seen them watch the less controversial, family-drama Hindi films or those that had gods and miracles in them. Bade Bhaisaab rarely spoke, and his conversations usually had to do with the land he farmed, the rain, the bullocks and pesticides. Didi spoke more than he, but mostly to her own children. Seema at times wondered about their love life, but had never dared to discuss it with Girish, who maintained decorum as far as his older brother was concerned. Seema didn't believe they were capable of romance, that they were capable of anything other than a mute acceptance of their lot, the mundane routine. Their presence at the theatre was more than a shock to her. It diminished her much anticipated outing, and the thought annoyed her much more than she cared to admit.

The movie began, but neither Girish nor Seema felt as enthusiastic about it as before. Despite the scantily clad gori mems, their attention was constantly being drawn towards the two dark figures sitting ahead. The movie was a thriller with a serial killer, and took off at a fast pace. Bullets flew, minor actors died, the heroine got chased by the killer. The chase grew scarier as the movie progressed. The hero chased the killer, but the latter kept escaping. The heroine escaped, and then, when she finally felt safe and was about to jump in bed with the hero, the killer turned up, and the excitement began all over again.

After a stressful time darting their eyes to the screen and back to the couple ahead, until both their eyes felt ready to burst, Girish and Seema relaxed sufficiently to cuddle and watch with more attention. Although they didn't understand a single word, the sheer movement of the movie carried them forward. Up ahead it seemed that the movie was having a similar effect on Bade Bhaisaab and Bhabiji. Girish could see their straight backs and the engrossed look on their faces. From time to time, Bade Bhaisaab swayed towards his wife and she reciprocated without a shred of shyness. Seema made eye contact with Girish. They sat watching with bated breaths as the movie reached its finale, and the rescued heroine and the chase-weary hero came together at the end of their travails for the final tryst in bed, where one could see up to their naked shoulders and no more. But suddenly Girish and Seema were forced to tear their eyes away from the screen. Transfixed, they watched Bhabiji fling her arms around Bade Bhaisaab. There was a collective audible gasp from all quarters of the hall. Girish clutched Seema's hand while her jaw dropped. Oblivious to the jeering and cheering in the hall, Bhabiji and Bhaisaab sat locked in a tight embrace, their lips sealed in an interminable kiss.

Girish did not wait for the lights to be switched on. Almost dragging Seema along, he fled. Once outside, they gulped mouthfuls of fresh air, but their relief was short-lived. Sanat appeared from nowhere, a cigarette dangling in the classic filmy pose of Rajnikanth from his mouth.

'Arrey guru! Bhaisaab and Bhabiji, waah! *Kya* kiss *kiya* yaar!' Sanat slapped Girish on the shoulder. He leered at Seema. The rest of Sanat's gang materialized as if by magic, sealing off any chance of an escape. Sanat offered him a cigarette, which Girish reluctantly accepted. Seema stood quietly on one side, hoping the men's bodies would hide her from the inquisitive stares of the women emerging from the hall. Everybody was discussing 'the kiss', as if that was all they had bought tickets to see, the movie having completely slipped from their minds. Some who were observing the little group that contained Girish and Seema pointed, waved and laughed knowingly. Mahadeo Pandey suddenly materialized. He nudged Girish and winked at Seema. The wink was a deliberate affront, but Girish was not in any state of mind to challenge Mahadeo.

People streamed past, carrying Bade Bhaisaab and Bhabiji in the flow. Their faces looked serene as they gracefully made their exit, as if nothing extraordinary had happened. No one jeered or winked at them. There was a slight pause in the hubbub, but the people just let them pass. Stunned by their equanimity, Seema followed Girish. She heard and noticed Sanat slapping Girish on the back as a mark of understanding. She saw the respectful look in Sanat's eyes as he stared at the kissing couple. Bhabiji and Bade Bhaisaab had, by that one act, become more dazzling than anything they had ever seen on the silver screen. Wondering about this new development in their lives, Girish covered the slow walk back to the side of the cinema hall where his scooter was parked. Demurely, Seema walked three feet behind him, her head bent and her face covered with her ghungat.

WORD AMONG POETS

I could have moved at that very instant, if I wanted to. I'm a verb after all. But I decided to wait for the right moment. Having been inert for so long, I wanted to savour it. I mean really savour it. So, here I am, narrating the events of the last poetry meeting She-poet ever attended. If I had fingers, I'd rub them in glee!

Someone had dropped me during a meeting. Thereafter, unnoticed, I slipped and slid around the table at the centre of the grey conference room, until I finally found a crack in the wood. I remained there, half-buried by a sticky blanket of grey-black erased words, each wrapped tightly in its casing of rubber. I was, for once, watching things unfold around me instead of being in the thick of it.

The conference room was inside a squat grey building, which was a cultural centre and library. There was also an auditorium. The other rooms were full of books and magazines, and soft piped music. Bulletins about cultural activities and happenings in the city were tacked on to felt-covered notice boards in the main hall. Everything inside was grey. The walls were grey. The tables were grey. The chairs were tubular steel with grey foam seats. Even the floor was a greasy grey colour. The conference room had a glossy calendar with a blood red arty print. It was the only bright thing in the room. But it was so arty that it failed to make things cheery.

It is a funny thing. I must have been in that room dozens of times, before my involuntary and sudden imprisonment within the table, but I had never bothered to look around properly. I had never truly seen the room and its inhabitants. I had never breathed in its atmosphere, so to speak. But once I was bundled up in the crack, I began to observe people closely. Perhaps that is why I was able to understand her the way others in the grey room never would.

She-poet was one among the two-dozen odd poets who gathered in the grey room every fortnight to read the poems they had written according to a theme chosen in the previous meeting. They assembled at six on the dot in the evening, which was close to dinner time for some of them. I watched them squirm when their stomachs grumbled, and cough to cover up for the sound. The others ignored these un-poetic sounds, and continued with the reading, discussing the merits and demerits of the poems, in soft cultured voices, careful not to irk one another, at least not too much. They reminded me of student ballet dancers doing pirouettes in front of a distinguished surprise-visitor at school.

Each poet brought a sheaf of poem-bearing papers. These were distributed to the members present, and extras were put away on one side of the table for latecomers. Some were habitually late. She-poet was one of them. She was late not because she was tardy by nature, but because she hated the city. The language was strange to her, even though they were all from the same country, and the locals treated her as if she was an unwanted foreigner. You could tell by the way she blundered in that she had not come out of her house until it was nearly time for the poetry reading to begin.

She was relatively, but only relatively, new to the city. She had lived in a cleaner, quieter place before, another country. She was used to wide expanses of greenery between her and other people. Some water had flowed under the bridge since, so now the 'being used to' bit was more of a mind thing than what being used to really meant. Nevertheless, She-poet remained faithfully wistful about her past expatriate status.

She had spent many years away, and after her return, felt overwhelmed by the blatant consumerism that had mushroomed all over her homeland. The country was now dirtier and more chaotic. She could not bear the sloppiness, the lack of civic sense in her fellow countrymen. It seemed to her that the new-found wealth had taught them nothing good; if anything, the sudden money was making everyone behave worse than ever.

She-poet found it difficult to come to terms with those who were less impressed by foreign things, and had travelled to more places in the world than she, without ever having been an expatriate. She was dismayed too, by the poverty on the pavements outside glittering hotels and malls, festering like the weeping sores of lepers. She-poet had many complaints. And though she took care not to voice them openly, her secret privations remained unresolved. And unknown to her, she was observed by others with pursed lips.

'I remember a land that was poor but genteel,' she once told the poets, after they had reacted blandly to one of her sugary patriotic poems.

A professor of English, sporting a French-cut beard and a thick provincial accent, held up the paper which contained her poem and said, 'So, according to you, that is the patrimony we deserve after being colonized?'

Before She-poet could think of a suitable retort, a member giggled and said that perhaps she was disappointed because they had progressed so much during the years she had lived abroad. There was a mocking silence as She-poet struggled to reply. The words were half-formed inside her head, but her tongue was too slow to lob them. A silver-haired lady with spectacles so thick that they looked like glass blinkers, and who was the de facto convener of the meetings, looked around owlishly for two or three seconds before reciting an absentee member's poem loudly. She-poet lost her chance, and inwardly fumed for the rest of the session.

Another time, another professor-poet, who, despite having a doctorate in English and being the principal of a suburban college, could barely write grammatically correct English, annoyed her so much that she didn't attend many sessions after that. He called himself a poet, wrote poetry and got it published. It was another matter that the books were shabbily printed by an obscure vanity press. Some gossiped that it was his own publishing house, set up to make money off desperate poets. Barely-literate-professor-poet also enjoyed bashing the erstwhile colonizers in his poetry and lectures. Nothing the ex-rulers did was good. But he had taken pains to get his degrees in English literature, albeit from questionable institutes, and had got his first job as a lecturer of English through much palm-greasing and bum-kissing. He was ingratiatingly nice to the other academics in the group. He seemed desperate to cling to a group of poets writing in the English language. The others knew that he had succeeded over the years because of his ability to hobnob with people with political clout, people who could fund and sanction arts grants and awards.

I watched Barely-literate-professor-poet glancing at She-poet every now and then. He took note of her Western clothes, and crisp British English. The glazed look in his eyes, which he took care to tone down, hidden from all except me, told me that he found her glamorous and sexy. Once, he had invited She-poet to his college function, but she had politely declined. Barely-literate-professor-poet avenged himself by writing a poem where he called members of her community sex-maniacs and sycophants of the British. He read the poem out at a meeting. She-poet could not follow the words of his poem because of his thin reedy voice and poor English diction. By the time the poem and its meaning sank in, it was too late. Everybody had hurriedly moved on to other poems. The poets of the grey room considered confrontations to be singularly un-poetic, so they took advantage of her lack of comprehension. It angered She-poet that they preferred to silently watch her being insulted. She assumed, not incorrectly, that because she was different from them, they would not stand up for her. She-poet stayed away for a long time. Owl-poet, finally, cajoled her. Numbers, though un-poetic, were needed at poetry meetings. She was relieved when She-poet returned.

There were some students among the poets as well, mostly young men who believed they were erudite. They attended the poetry sessions haphazardly. They forgot to bring the right poems, and sometimes they ignored the theme completely. They insisted on reading out their poems twice. They demanded feedback and argued fiercely. Everybody tolerated them because nothing in art is lively or lovely without the exuberance of young blood.

Their most vociferous supporter was an old man with a head like a polished mahogany doorknob. His doorknob head sat loosely on his neck and nodded all the time, like a wooden doll with a spring neck. Doorknob-head-poet wrote long tapering poems with sprigs of elegant words buttonholed between lines. But perhaps due to his hushed confidential voice, everybody nodded off when he read. Afterwards, they all took care to praise the elegance of his poems whether they remembered them or not.

Every now and then, a woman with dirty teeth and toenails and smelly sweat-stained armpits, working as an executive somewhere, walked in to attend. Executive-poet, despite her tackiness and lack of hygiene, had an engineering degree followed by a diploma in management. She was self-assured and knew exactly what she wanted in life, and how to go about getting it. And when she made a catty remark, no one heard her except the person it was meant for.

She-poet, who used to wear cycling shorts to the park and formal flat-front trousers with collared shirts during client meetings for her freelance writing assignments when she lived abroad, once sashayed in, wearing a maxi-length slit skirt. She usually wore longish tops over slim-fit trousers, but that day, she wanted to be her 'old' self. Executive-poet saw her and murmured that *she* would never have worn such an outfit. She-poet pretended not to hear her at first, in accordance with her sophisticated expatriate image. A little later, it occurred to her that she could have easily replied,

'Oh, but *you* shouldn't. *You* would never be able to carry it off!' But this cutting rejoinder sprouted in her head a few seconds too late. She avenged herself by pointing out, on the side, to Owl-poet that Executive-poet stank and lacked class, and that her English had a provincial accent, however faint. Owl-poet continued with the poetry meeting as if she had heard nothing.

Later, Owl-poet observed to She-poet that Executive-poet was 'impatiently ambitious'. After that, she told Executive-poet that She-poet took things too personally. 'Don't bother her too much, she is like that only!'

Executive-poet believed she resembled the women in Ravi Varma paintings. She had once mentioned it to She-poet who had smirked before turning away. Executive-poet told the gathered poets that she could not attend the meetings regularly, because being higher up in the corporate ladder meant that she had very little time, which was not quite true.

I often caught Executive-poet looking disdainful for exactly half a second, when a poem was read out. She wrote richly flavoured poems herself, and had been published in two or three prestigious publications. Nevertheless, she liked to keep at least a tip of one of her fingers in all things related to literature, as she was an aspiring novelist, and you never knew when a person would turn out to be useful. She was both envious of and fascinated by She-poet, and dreamed of the day she would become a successful expatriate herself.

This motley group of poets included a few housewives and retired government servants. The housewife–poets had more time to spare now that their children had grown up and husbands were retired. The retired-government-servant-poets had nothing but time on their hands. This group of people formed the backbone of the poetry meetings in the grey room. They wrote with care. Sometimes they wrote with too much care, scratching out each printed or photocopied word diligently before filling up the blank space above the scratched-out word with another. They heeded all the comments and made pencil marks in the margins. They offered carefully phrased opinions.

Everybody loved them. But not all among the housewives and retiree poets were innocent. One of them, who hardly said a word and always jotted down the comments, knew a retired judge who used his position to become the president of a cash-rich international poetry association. The association held a conference in a posh hotel in the city, and invited her to speak. Quiet as a mouse, one of the house-wife poets, kept the news to herself. The poets of the grey room learnt about it when they saw the pictures in the newspapers, and were displeased.

In spite of these hiccups and sly acts, the meetings carried on. Not everybody was poetic all the time. Not everybody was able to attend all the time, except for Owl-poet, who loved poetry and gossip too much to miss even a day.

The poets were oblivious to my presence, even when I made their lines ripple with energy. This should have annoyed me, I know. But verbs have no egos. We do not take revenge on our users by suddenly becoming passive unless, of course, we are made to, against our will, let me hasten to add. I am quite capable of turning into a wallflower when there is an adverb overload. Actually 'wallflower' is a mild word. In order to truly understand how I feel, you have to imagine being Gulliver, lying helpless and inert on the sand, but with his entire faculties alert, every strand of hair and every skinfold tied to the ground.

Verbs have staunch defenders among poets, contrary to popular belief. She-poet and Executive-poet were verb defenders. Doorknob-head-poet, Professor-French-cut-poet and some poets from the housewives and retirees group also looked after us—me—well. The worst offenders were the students. One of them even had a book of poems published, which did not sell a single copy. Some of the poets whispered that his father, who had paid for the poetry publication, also knew a number of big shots in the media. His poetry books were neatly tucked away on the shelves of a number of libraries in the city. He was also invited to book events and launches. He was disliked by them. He felt intimidated by She-poet. He displayed nonchalance by growing a triangle-shaped beard no bigger than the big toe on his chin.

His beard was a source of irritation for the senior members. It looked like a hairy mole, a vulgar mole that took delight in reminding them of outraged female modesty. The gentlemen were constantly distracted by it. The ladies ignored it as best as they could. She-poet secretly itched to run her razor over his 'chinny-chin-chin'. She also wanted to slap Chinny-chin-chin-poet, holding his neck with one hand while her other hand went phlath-phlath-phlath over his smooth cheeks. She had visualized it many times. In my opinion, that would have been strong active action! As a verb, I cannot but applaud even the thought of such an action.

One unprepossessing summer day, She-poet hailed her usual taxi, hating the city's smoky air that constantly shoved itself into her cab. Like before, she had started out at the very last minute. There was a political rally that day, so the traffic had coagulated at every road junction. She-poet cursed the city. She chipped a polished finger nail on the door of the cab when she got out. A small pebble from the gravelled path to the grey room attached itself to the sole of her sandal. She-poet cursed herself for wearing open-toed sandals instead of her usual clean-feet-preserving pumps. The receptionist in the lobby was new, and failed to recognize She-poet. She waited as the receptionist took her time looking up her particulars in the registration book. By the time She-poet entered the grey room, all the poems had been read and discussed. Everybody was in the relaxed mood that comes with knowing that soon they would be home, eating dinner and watching television with their families. They were discussing the theme for the next meeting when She-poet burst in.

'Sorry,' she said. 'I had to wait at the . . .'

'Oh. But we didn't,' said one of the student-poets rudely.

Everybody tittered politely.

'Sit down,' said Owl-poet. 'At least you came.'

'We were discussing the theme for our next meeting,' said Professor-French-cut-poet.

'How about "tardiness" or just "tardy",' quipped Chinny-chin-chin-poet.

'The dear belated but not departed?' suggested Executive-poet softly.

More giggles followed. The air was tense with apprehension. Some members smiled nervously. Some watched in alarm as She-poet clenched and unclenched her jaw. 'Actually,' said a retired-government-servant-poet, clearing his throat, 'actually, I was thinking about "word" itself as a theme. You know word, wordiness, wordish, even as a verb—worded, wording, see?'

'That's an interesting idea,' said Doorknob-head-poet, smiling encouragingly.

They thought about the new theme, and the room relaxed in the silence that followed. But She-poet was still furious with the taunts. She shuffled through her papers as if looking for something. She put the papers away and opened her handbag. She took out another paper from it. A smile bloomed on her face, plumping up her cheeks.

'I think that's a splendid idea,' she said. 'Word as a theme is perfect.'

'Really?' said Chinny-chin-chin-poet with an eyebrow cocked at her. 'Why do you say that?'

'You have a poem written on the theme, already. Right?' said Executive-poet slyly.

'Yes, I do!' cried She-poet in triumph. 'Call it providence. And you know what?' she said turning first towards Barely-literate-professor-poet, and then towards Chinny-chin-chin-poet. 'You two were my inspiration.'

Barely-literate-professor-poet immediately looked wary. He kept his head down to avoid any confrontation.

'I'm flattered,' drawled Chinny-chin-chin-poet.

'Don't be!' snapped She-poet.

Owl-poet started protesting that she would have to wait for the next meeting, but She-poet ignored her. She began to read the poem aloud in her ringing elocution voice:

GUT WORD

Sit still
for an instant.
Be quiet
and hold

your stomach in.
Imagine a fart
growing
like poetic wind.
Stretching,
Elongating,
into an enduring
consonant.
With such cutting-air clarity
that it rises sharply
and impales
the following
vowel.
The vowel explodes
instantly.
Now imagine a poem
growing
Like a fart.

After what seemed to be an interminable moment, Owl-poet said that she thought the poem was humorous. The retired-government-servant-poets looked baffled. The housewife-poets giggled softly. Barely-literate-professor-poet shifted in his seat. Professor-French-cut-poet stroked his chin. Student-poets snickered. Chinny-chin-chin-poet left his chair and walked up to She-poet. He slapped her on the back playfully.

'Wowzie! You rock, girl!' he said, in his best American accent.

'But you don't! Buffoon!'

Right then and there, She-poet slapped Chinny-chin-chin-poet back. Hard. On his cheek, close to the vulgar triangle. Her slap carried with it the weight of her anger, not just for Chinny-chin-chin-poet and Barely-literate-professor-poet, but also for the rest of them—the city, her chipped fingernail, the gravel in her sandal, and her diminished expatriate status . . . The hurricane of her fury whirled around the room, ruffling Executive-poet's oily hair among other things.

Owl-poet's lips formed a perfect 'O', The housewife-poets had their hands clasped over their mouths. Professor-French-cut-poet had already risen from his chair as if to barricade the storm with his broad body. But the retired-government-servant-poets remained sitting as if they were made of stone.

Chinny-chin-chin-poet spluttered, looked shocked, and made an aggressive move towards She-poet. But Professor-French-cut-poet quickly caught him. Unspoken things whooped and whistled around the room. And then, there was deathly silence.

I thought the silence in the grey room would never end, but it did. Finally, and calamitously, just after She-poet made her exit. I correctly sensed that this time her exit was for good. If people noticed how her cheeks flamed, red like a pair of tomatoes, and then turned pale again, they ignored it, preferring instead to surround Chinny-chin-chin-poet. I looked around me, at them. I decided that right or wrong, She-poet was sure to be a more interesting host. So, I jumped, straight on to her squared-up shoulders, just as she opened the door. It closed behind her with the judder of stressed-out glass. And that I knew was the herald for a new season. But only for the two of us.

PATCHWORK

Joy ignores the tension in the seams of his pants. Peace had darned them so carefully, with near invisible stitches, as if she had been sewing a patch of her own skin. She had even run a strengthening line along the seams with her sewing machine. He knows they'll hold. No matter what.

Peace's face seems to float by in the breeze as he climbs, and Joy shuts his eyes for a second to hold the image.

Their names were given to them by the padre who had baptized them. Perhaps the good Father had been struck by the couple's aura of endless hope. Perhaps he'd seen the rhythmic possibilities of their native names turned into English in a moment of drollery. And so, Joydev Chaki had become Joy Dave Chaki. Priyoshi Chaki had turned into Peace Priscilla Chaki. And their son Mihir became Merry Henry Chaki. But their daughter, born after the conversion, was christened Delight Daisy

Chaki straightaway. Two brand new English names, not transformed ones like theirs. The family calls her Deelightee, almost singing her name to the dimpled-with-happiness little girl.

The framed church certificate looks like a picture. The picture of a happy family. And why not? Happiness is all they care about, regardless of the gods they entrust their care to. Joy still harbours some guilt though. He has memories of his mother placing a hand, warmed from the flame of a lamp, on his head, a blessing carried over from their household deity after her evening prayers. It is there within him, as vivid and comforting as the pot of hot rice she used to set before him every day, insisting that he ate his fill, before she herself did.

Joy doesn't consciously think about the conversion. But the thought somehow makes its presence felt. Niggling him like the last pinworm of his childhood, too stubborn to succumb to the bitter medicine concocted by the local herbalist, and tenaciously clinging on to the ends of his innards, making him squirm every now and then.

Peace has little patience with sentimental things, but she understands Joy's unspoken dilemma. She will never throw the deity away, never slam the door on a talisman her husband relies on, however blasphemous. The good fathers of their church, and their fellow Christians don't need to know, that's all.

Joy grasps the brush with his teeth. He flings a sinewy arm upwards to catch the horizontal bar of the rope-and-bamboo ladder, lifting his leg up at the same time, foot curving around the bar in a precarious hold. The contraption sways every time he moves, and he has to steady himself repeatedly. He could be a dressed-up circus monkey for all they—the overseers of the construction company he works for—cared. Joy frowns to concentrate. He can't afford not to. Not with the hard ground below. Not with the merciless sky shimmering above him. Minuscule dark spots appear before his eyes the instant he looks away. Joy stares at the structure in front. Its solidity reassures him. He swings himself up but without the easy grace of an orangutan, and reaches the portion of the building he and his colleagues are to work on today.

It's a risky job, with no compensation or insurance. He's not entitled to severance pay, because he is a contractual labourer. He doesn't even belong to any workers' union. He is in God's hands. A specific, round-bellied deity, in fact, carved from stone. A God with a benign smile beneath a curly beard. And he sits on Peace's alcove, with no visible signs of worship, like vermillion and incense ash, upon his person. He is the one Joy avoids eye contact with, pretending to adjust his trousers or do a button on his shirt, hoping his neglected protector doesn't think he is being deliberately impertinent.

Now Joy keeps his eyes determinedly up, even when he feels blinded by the hot sun. He dare not close them against the heat. What if he sees the ground spinning when he opens them? His canvas shoes with the worn-to-a-wafer thin rubber soles squeak and slide against the smooth bamboo bar. He is used to getting teased for the shoes; the others shimmy up in their bare feet, but Joy wears socks and shoes, and a colourful handkerchief tied around his neck too. He is an ardent fan of Rajinikanth, the action-hero who rose from humble beginnings. He often hums songs from the megastar's movies.

A breeze comes along and plays a game of tug of war with the coir rope. Joy hangs on. He's been doing the same job for several years now. His routine never falters. The hours never vary. The buildings change with every new assignment, but in the end, they all look the same.

Joy is known for his neatness, the quality of his work. He has the aura of an educated man about him, even though he couldn't finish school. His colleagues find him friendly but reserved. They sense a certain hunger in him. They find him fastidious when it comes to his attire, in spite of the paint stains. And even though they have never met Peace face-to-face, they know all about her talent for sewing. Some of them have also seen Joy on his way to church on Sundays, nattily dressed, flanked by a pair of small children in cleverly put-together patchwork clothes, and a woman, who they assume must be Peace.

The tin-roofed single-room shack, with a shaded courtyard, the size of a bedspread for a kitchen, and a community bathroom a few metres beyond, is both home and workshop. Here, Peace sweeps up the bits of cloth and fluff into separate piles. She uses the fluff as stuffing for the cloth toys she makes, a side business of hers. The bits of cloth will go into a big bag, for the endless patchwork things in her home. She sews small pieces of cloth together into a large workable piece, which she then cuts into shape and stitches again. Leftovers are precious, because her customers usually need only their shirt collars turned and pants let out. Some customers remember to ask for the leftover cloth, and she hands the pieces over without a word. They're all in the same boat after all. Some let her have them, departing with a knowing smirk. Peace ignores them, bending down grim-faced to her machine, and carries on.

Some openly snigger when they see the girl and boy walking hand in hand in their motley clothes. 'Look at our fashion models!' They call. 'Look. Look! High fashion!'

Peace holds her head high. Joy's clothes have never had to submit themselves to the parsimony of her shears and thread, except for the near invisible darned parts, the tactfully renewed collar. He is better-looking and better- dressed than the other men. Her trusty second-hand Singer, donated to her by the church, has never disrespected her man.

Peace dreams of a house of their own, built from scratch by Joy. She visualizes him leaning against the roof, hammering away or wielding a brush. Merry and Deelightee running about, making a game of it, handing him tools, a mug of tea. She sees herself squatting before a portable coal stove, stirring chicken curry, chiefly made up of the butcher's discards, sold for a pittance to customers like her and dog owners, but with three good pieces thrown in, bought with money carefully extracted from her own nest egg. A man has to eat, and so do his children.

Peace thinks of her friends who work in high-rise apartments in the city. They return home with plastic bags of leftover food. The delicate stomachs of the rich cannot digest what's been sitting in the refrigerator for more than a week. Merry and Deelightee have told her about the meals their friends get to eat every now and then. But Joy would never let her do a maid's job. And Peace's heart swells with pride. Her Joy is different. He doesn't come home swaying and cursing after a binge at the toddy shop. He doesn't beat her. He doesn't gamble. He never visits bad women. Peace purses her lips. She knows what they are called, but will not sully her house by naming them.

She knows her friends envy her. She's been careful not to tell them about their escape in the dead of night from one identity to another. From the dirt tracks of their village in Midnapore to the outskirts of bustling Kolkata, their journey had been long and arduous after the quick and quiet ceremony. How Joy, originally a farming lad, had doggedly taught himself new tricks and skills. And how

Peace had focused on honing her natural talent for sewing as soon as she had got her precious machine.

Peace studies the two-metre-long pieces she had picked up from a yard sale at a store. They are almost identical in colour and texture. A string of sweat beads lines her upper lip. A pinch of creativity is all she needs to turn them into a decent shirt for Joy. She takes a nub of marking wax and taps it on the small worktable as she ponders about the design.

A sudden hullaballoo interrupts her reverie. What she sees outside her door knocks the breath out of her lungs, leaving her gasping. It's Nuruddin, Joy's friend, bloodied and dishevelled, surrounded by what appears to be their entire locality. An accident at the site, something about rotten coir ropes, with one man already dead, one critical, two, like Nuruddin, not so critical, and one hanging on for dear life. The information pours out piecemeal, in a jumble of incoherent words. She steadies herself to take in the worst, and then collapses on her doorstep.

Minutes later, Peace is racing towards the building. She touches the cross swinging from a loop of black twine around her neck and simultaneously squeezes the stone idol in her closed fist. She'd remembered to pluck it from the alcove when she hastily locked the house and ran out. Thankfully, the children are still at school. Anger wells up towards the God in her fist. She is certain he is taking revenge because they switched loyalties, at least publicly.

Why are their gods so unreasonable? In this country, changing track is just another means of surviving. Since he's God, can't he be more understanding? More forgiving?! What kind of God is he? She hopes the quieter one, the one that dangles perennially from a cross, her self-installed patron of her tailoring business, will not let her down. She prays to him, and at the same time, quite unconsciously, brings up her idol-gripped fist to her breast. Her eyes dart around for a fire engine. There is none in sight. Her feet fly over the hot dusty road. By the time she reaches the site, her rib muscles are stiff with pain and she can barely breathe. She doesn't speak to anyone as she frantically searches for her Joy. Finally, she sees a familiar shape on the coir ropes, dangling in the air.

Joy looks strange, like a puppet whose puppeteer, bored of his trade, has absconded. The sight of him wrings out a hysterical laugh from Peace's throat. He is approximately forty feet above ground, enough to get himself killed if he loses grip. Some of Joy's colleagues and friends are standing on a balcony close by. They are shouting encouraging words, asking him to try and use his body like a pendulum to swing towards them. The building is incomplete and some of its parts don't even have walls. The balcony doesn't have railings yet, so the men are holding on to a pillar and extending their arms towards Joy.

To Peace, it seems like the earth's gravity has suddenly increased tenfold, and time has flattened itself into a thin sheet. She feels certain that they will soon, all of them together, be crushed into nothingness. She wills herself to fight against the sensation. Like a swimmer in a choppy sea desperately surfacing for air, she tries to lift herself from the ground, flinging her arms skywards with a force she never knew she had. The deity in her hand flies out with impatient velocity.

The small ping-pong ball-like thing, weighty for its size, arcs through the air higher and higher until it grazes Joy's cheek, startling him. Joy releases the rope as he tries, on reflex, to catch the lobbed missile. A second too late, he realizes his mistake and plunges below. Horror robs Peace of voice and movement. But there is a crowd of men ahead of her, closer to the building, immediately below him. Their unified 'aaahaaaahaaiii' waxes like the ululation of devotees as they move with the fluidity of a boneless beast towards her falling Joy.

Through the surging heads and crowd of bodies Peace catches glimpses of a patchwork sheet held up by many hands, making up a large hammock of many colours. The sheet or bedspread or whatever it is seems luminously familiar. But she cannot remember stitching it. Questions hop about in her mind. Did someone copy her idea, then? And does that mean that there is another tailor in their locality? Was that why her business had been dwindling lately? Or was it really one of her own bedspreads? A piece that she may have sold to one of her neighbours during a particularly tight month? But who had brought it here? Was it still strong enough?

A part of her mind is amazed that she can stand there and think of so many little things. Another part is numb, not daring to articulate the fear thrashing about her stomach like a snake that has its head caught in a rat trap. Another ululation resonates, making the stone-hard panic in Peace's breast unbearable. She gazes stupidly at the patchwork spread. The seconds stretch treacherously before her.

And then suddenly, in authentic Rajinikanth style, there is her Joy, rolling on the cloth amidst the shouts and hurrahs of his mates, and the distant scream of the now unnecessary fire engine. Peace pushes her way through the crowd of sweaty excited people. She goes up to her Joy and retrieves him. And, he, trying hard to be normal, ends up smiling nervously at everyone around, the fingers of his right hand still fused around the idol. Involuntary shivers run through his back every now and then. He stands on shaky legs, barely aware of Peace who is holding him.

Enough excitement for the day, Peace decides. She takes him straight home and shuts the door on her neighbours. She wants them both to be calm before Merry and Deelightee return.

Later in the day, after everybody has been scrubbed clean, and after they've eaten their afternoon meal, they dress up in their Sunday best and slip away to church. Peace and Joy walk, hands linked, holding a child each on either side, forming a little chain, like the linked daddy-mummy-brother-sister kite-paper family Merry had cut out for Deelightee last Sunday. Peace and Joy move together, their steps eager with renewed hope. Their children hop on either side, excited about this sudden outing.

The cool and quiet interiors of the tall stone building are calming. They kneel down together before Mother Mary's statue holding the infant Jesus in the crook of her arm, her other hand raised in a benediction, eyes as serene as lotus buds. After that, they kneel before the crucifix above the pulpit where they receive the holy communion every Sunday. And then, they make the children slip coins of small denominations into the slit on top of the donation box, a fistful each. Merry and Deelightee take their time to insert the coins, listening for the clink of falling metal with shining eyes.

When they come out, they are greeted by a blushing young evening. Cool air from a faraway ocean drifts into their city. The scent of newly blossoming night flowers spreads quiet cheer around them. The atmosphere feels almost festive, and they laugh together like any other family on a vacation would. Merry and Deelightee have an ice-cream cone each. Their faces are glowing because of this unprecedented treat. Sensing the mood, they offer licks and bites of their treat to Peace and Joy, and the parents taste the cool creamy luxury gingerly, almost kissing the frozen confectionery, as if they were Jesus's feet.

Even later, when evening has succumbed to night, Joy and Peace stand before the idol in the alcove. Joy bends his head ever so slightly, his eyes closing for a second in an imperceptible gesture of gratitude.

When the night has lengthened into a stiller creature, long after the children have fallen asleep, Peace and Joy ease their bodies away from each other, with the quietness of long practice. The languor that comes after deep physical pleasure melts and merges slowly into tender conversation, both verbal and tactile.

Peace places the two swatches of cloth on Joy, one on each shoulder. She checks the texture of the fabric against his skin, the drape of it on his torso. He sniffs the crisp smell of new cloth, and slides his fingers across its smoothness. They giggle softly. Then they cry a little and wipe away each other's tears with the pieces of cloth. They pull each other close again, breathing through the fabric, stalling each other's involuntary shiver with their arms as their nerve cells relive the cold chasm that had opened up without warning in the midst of their lives.

Sleep has, until now, eluded Peace and Joy. The whites of their eyes beam out towards each other in the smoky darkness. An unspoken determination pulsates between them. A new fierceness burns in their hearts, fanning their mutual will to survive, their need to cut through the walls before them and to hold their dreams in their own hands. Right now, though, they are too exhausted to dwell upon fresh possibilities and visualize the desires raging within their hearts. The gentle, trustful breathing of their children on the thin mattress next to their own creates a soothing, almost lulling rhythm. Sleep, at long last, does come to them, sauntering slowly into their personal space, catlike in its stealth. This time though, they are ready, even eager to welcome their tardy visitor. And when they close their eyes, it is with the gratitude of boon-seekers.

IT COMES FROM URANUS

The last straw, according to Sarbani, was her passing gas in the car. Uttam was driving, with Sarbani in the passenger seat next to him and Ritu in the back seat. Sarbani wrinkled her nose and complained loudly to make it obvious. She exchanged glances with Uttam and rolled down the window. Ritu had a beatific smile, her eyes staring at the darkness outside. This was not the first time. Sarbani concluded she didn't respect them. She didn't care what they thought.

'I can't believe this!' she fumed. 'How dare she?!'

'She's an Indian-born American rustic,' said Uttam. 'Doesn't she remind you of a ding from Free School Street?'

Ritu, or Rits, as Sarbani had been affectionately calling her, had bright burgundy hair. She noted that the hair could have matched Ritu's light green-brown eyes if she wasn't so swarthy, and Sarbani had involuntarily glanced at

164

her own nearly yellow complexion. Yes, she did have that Anglo look about her. Nevertheless, she had an air about her, as if the colour of her eyes gave her American passport greater legitimacy. She had talked about how the chap at the immigration counter at New York had remarked on her eyes.

'There I was Bani, with just $20 in my pocket. Just back from Kolkata. I didn't know if my citizenship had been approved or not. But no choice. How long can a married daughter stay with her parents? I mean, I had responsibilities. I told myself, heck, I've got my return ticket. Something will turn up.'

Ritu was proud of her struggles and eager to talk about them. By the second evening and third bottle of wine (expensive wine, as Uttam whispered later when they were alone, referring to the $30 each Cabernet Sauvignon Blanc and the Pinot Noir he had picked up on his return trip from the UK a few months back), they knew about her drunken encounter with an equally drunk American guy in college.

'Nothing happened,' she had quickly clarified. 'He took me to his place in his car. Both of us were so . . . I could barely walk! I saw a picture of this woman on his bedside table and asked who she was. He straightened up then. And I said, "Can you please take me back?" An angel must have been looking after me that day. He drove me back to my dorm, you know.'

'No angel. He was a good guy,' said Sarbani.

Ritu told them how, before her Polish-American ex-husband and the father of her two girls, she'd been married off to a psycho Indian guy by her cousin who lived there, the same cousin who had sponsored her. She related her great escape story. And how she'd worked as a live-in nanny for a couple of years. Her first real job.

'They were so good to me. Young couple with three kids. They helped me. Gave me their old car. Put me in touch with a good divorce lawyer, cheap. You know, Bani,' she said confidentially, 'the whiteys have helped me much more. I'm proud to be a Bengali, but I don't know . . . Can't relate to the Bong community. Went to a Durga Puja one time with my cousin. Didn't know who to talk to there.'

She had trouble with Douglas too. He was a professor of philosophy and an Indophile—her words. They had met at a commune she had landed up in after taking a wrong turn. This was after she'd finished her masters in physiotherapy or psychotherapy or geriatric therapy—Sarbani never got the hang of Ritu's degrees—and begun her first full-time job.

'Was it love at first sight?'

Ritu shrugged. 'Not for me. I mean, I wasn't so much into white guys, you know. But he kind of grew on me. Anyway, he was very persuasive. I think he wanted to fall in love with an Indian woman. He knew so much about Kali! Then I guess the exotic appeal waned. He didn't like the food I cooked. And I hate blue cheese. Yuck!'

Most of Ritu's American friends on Facebook were white or black. The Indian ones were all old schoolmates, like Sarbani. But unlike the others, they were not old 'old' schoolmates. Sarbani had met Ritu at a Protestant school in Kolkata which they both had attended. It was a frumpy institution, nearly as old as Kolkata. Sarbani didn't have a clear memory about her own reason for going there after her convent school, where she'd been a boarder. Perhaps it was because there were fewer choices for those who needed hostel accommodation. Ritu used to be a day-scholar. She was also from a convent, but had lived with her maternal aunt and uncle throughout her school years. She had stories to share about her abuse by her cousin brother and uncle too. She told Sarbani how the whole thing had come out at a shrink's clinic; it had literally burst out of her. Douglas had insisted she see one. He had hugged her later, really tight, and said he understood why she was so fucked up.

'The whole world seems to have molested your friend,' Uttam observed afterwards.

Sarbani was more inclined to be sympathetic. But that was before the scene Ritu created at the crafts fair, and her wind-passing marathon on the way back from Mahabalipuram. Afterwards, she wondered how they had become friends. She didn't know anything about Ritu. And Ritu had assumed that she came from the same kind of backward and therefore equally ambitious family like her own. It annoyed Sarbani that Ritu didn't know she was familiar with all the British rock bands, had been listening to them since her schooldays as a matter of fact. Or the fact that she had played squash and gone swimming at the club in her town. And that they had jamming sessions and disco nights there. Ritu also didn't know that she had grown up in an environment where many white people lived, were their neighbours in fact, or that her mom played canasta and whist with them along with other Indian women. What was more, Ritu wasn't even aware that ham and eggs had been her staple breakfast and they'd had turkey for Christmas, while Ritu had returned every day to her provincial Kolkata suburb, narrow streets with open drains, power cuts and hard smelly water. They must have eaten from steel plates on the floor, Sarbani told Uttam, when Ritu left for the airport, shortly after creating a small sentimental scene at the car park in front of a bemused taxi driver.

In retrospect, Ritu had been annoying right from the start. From the excessive gifts, and that huge bottle of Jim Beam—did she think they couldn't afford good whisky? She expected them to be impressed with Jim Beam? Uttam had shown her their little bar, chock-a-block with Talisker, Macallan, Glenmorangie, Glenlivet, Glenfiddich and Jameson. They kept Teachers' and Black Dog for everyday drinking. Then there was their stash of Hennessy and Martell, Bombay Sapphire and Beefeater. And of course, Absolut vodka jostling for space with a bottle of Old Monk rum. Their bar was good by any international standards.

Her 600-litre double-door fridge had a whole shelf filled with wine bottles. They planned to buy an electric cooler for their wine collection soon. The kind that shops kept for storing cold drinks.

Ritu didn't seem to notice any of it. Not the air-conditioned rooms and hall, the fans and geysers in the bathrooms, the porcelain soap dishes and shampoo dispensers. She didn't comment on Sarbani's crystal collection, or the nearly four-feet wide almost wafer-thin television. She noticed nothing except for the dishwasher, and that too obliquely. She said that it was more hygienic to wash dishes by machine than hand on account of the steaming hot water. Sarbani agreed, even though she used the dishwasher only when the maid didn't turn up or for washing her fine china and glassware.

Ritu had emptied a bag full of goodies on the very first visit. After that, she kept thrusting something or the other into Sarbani's reluctant hands. Once, she had even clasped a white metal and plastic charm bracelet around Sarbani's wrist, a thing the latter would never wear. Hadn't she noticed her diamond earrings and pendant? The large star ruby ring she wore, and of course, her solitaire? She wished she'd told her to her face that she didn't wear artificial jewellery. Ritu had refused her without hesitation when Sarbani had tried to give her the top she'd lent her to wear. And this was another annoying thing; another rustic quality. Why did she need to borrow clothes? It was not as if she hadn't brought enough. Two suitcases full for less than a week. But that typical suburban Bengali habit of putting on other people's clothes hadn't left her despite her three decades overseas. And then she had the nerve to say that she wouldn't ever wear the top in California.

Ritu had retained other telltale signs of her origins. She wore an oval-shaped coral on a silver ring for some astrological reason. She said she was a *manglik*, which was why men felt intimidated and left her. Uttam had guffawed when they were alone.

'I thought manglik was a Hindi-belt thing. Where did a fish-curry-and-rice Bong like her start to believe in these things?'

Sarbani wondered how Ritu had been able to intimidate her white husband. Ritu confided one morning that during one of their quarrels, when her mother was visiting, Douglas had told Ritu to return to India. Her mother had walked up to him then, and said, 'Doglaaas, why you say haar go back? You not breeng haar here.' Ritu, mimicking her mother's broken English had sounded indulgent, not ashamed. She was proud of her mom. Proud that she had helped her family financially, and even settled her younger brother in the US.

'Does he visit you often?'

'Him? No. He wants to be independent. He's being kept by an older white woman, literally. She knows what he's up to. Him, and his used car business.'

Her Mercedes was a deal he had worked out for her. Sarbani gathered that they were in touch, but the brother didn't want his big sister's help any more. Her daughters were grown and were living with their respective boyfriends. They didn't speak Bengali, and hadn't hooked up with Indian boys. When she got a craving for Bengali food, she cooked rice and potatoes, mixed it with salt and butter and sometimes a hard-boiled egg. Cooking a Bengali meal for one person was too much hassle and the leftovers seemed to last an age. There was nowhere she could get real and proper Bengali food even though there were many Indian restaurants.

She didn't pray, she said, but wore a cross on a thin silver chain, and kept a framed picture of Saradama and Ramakrishnadeb and another of Kalima on an alcove tucked away in an unobtrusive corner of her large house with a swimming pool, inherited from Douglas as part of her divorce settlement. She had girlfriends who had helped her 'do the divorce'. Ritu had never learnt to swim. Her horoscope said she would die in water.

Sarbani dutifully took her sightseeing to Kapaleeshwarar Temple, one of the few that allowed foreigners, not that anyone would be the wiser as far as Ritu was concerned. After that, they went to the craft exhibition at Valluvar Kottam, and that was where Ritu misbehaved.

One minute they were admiring terracotta planters and pots, and the next thing she knew, Ritu was furiously rummaging in her large bag, looking sterner by the second.

'I've been robbed,' she announced.

Sarbani flushed. 'Oh God! How? When? What . . .what happened?'

'My wallet,' Ritu hissed. 'It had my travellers' cheques. My dollars. Credit card. All gone!'

The travellers' cheque part had Sarbani flummoxed for a minute. That was so last century. Didn't she have an international debit card? But her announcement had caused a stir. A few people now surrounded them. Sympathetic, ashamed, curious. Sarbani was mortified. Ritu with her foreign diction was a curiosity. Some kind people directed them to a police station nearby.

Before they left, Ritu muttered loud enough for all to hear and Sarbani to cringe: 'Anything can happen in this country. Den of thieves!'

Sarbani harried her driver to be quick; he drove on the wrong side of the road in his haste. Ritu didn't notice, but Sarbani wanted to duck her head. Worse was to follow. The police station was almost vacant. It was lunch hour. Ritu made a face.

'Nobody works in this country! How does it run?'

A constable looked at Ritu, pondered something and ushered them upstairs. They were in luck. The deputy police commissioner was visiting the station that day. Sarbani explained that her American friend's wallet had been stolen. The officer looked grave.

'Madam, please describe it,' he said gently.

'What is there to *describe*? I didn't see the thief. Does anyone speak English here?'

The officer glanced at Sarbani. Embarrassed and flustered, she apologized.

'My friend is a guest in this country . . . My guest. Sir, sorry to trouble you. As her host, I am ashamed she got robbed.'

'Yes, I know,' he replied kindly. 'Her English is also very different from ours.'

'Yes, yes, sir. You are right,' Sarbani nodded vigorously. The head nod, which she had picked up during her five-year stay in Chennai, made her look like a bobblehead. Uttam told her often enough that this particular head nod thing was unheard of in Bengal.

'Please ask her to fill out a form.' He waved a hand and the constable rushed forward with one. 'Don't worry. We will do our best,' he paused, before adding, 'I know how you feel.'

Sarbani thanked him and the constable profusely. Ritu remained stone-faced. She jabbed at the form, a deep frown ridging her brow. They returned home in silence while Ritu filled the car with silent stink bombs from time to time.

The first thing she did was to throw open the cupboard Sarbani had half-emptied for her and pull out her things. After ten minutes of rummaging, she emerged victorious.

'It was here all the time. I'd taken the other one by mistake. That one has my small cash.'

Sarbani itched to slap her then and there.

'Congrats!' She punched in the number the constable had given her on her cell phone.

'Hello? Egmore police station? Uh, I was there this afternoon with my American friend? Uh yes, yes. No, no trouble. You all have been so kind. Sorry to trouble all of you. Very sorry. No. No. I mean my friend made a mistake. Yes. Big mistake. She found her wallet. Thank you, thank you. So sorry.'

'It's too late to go back, right?' said Ritu.

'Yes. Would you like some tea?'

'Don't mind if I do.'

It didn't take long for Ritu to start again—how she loved the smell of coffee in the mornings, how she just had to have her blah blah blah latte.

They ate dinner outside, at an expensive Thai restaurant, which Sarbani insisted on paying for. Ritu discovered how pricey India was only when she took them out for a treat at a five-star restaurant near Mahabalipuram the next day. Uttam wanted to pay, but she would have none of it. Afterwards, she proclaimed that she'd never spent a hundred dollars on ordinary food in California. Perhaps that was why she was gassy all the way back.

Ritu accused Sarbani of being testy the day before she left. Sarbani hadn't realized that she had been responding curtly. She wasn't aware that she'd been given a chance to speak at all. But Ritu was probably right. Sarbani was finding her intolerable and it was obvious. Everything Ritu said, did or wore got on her nerves.

She complimented her cooking and said Sarbani cooked just the way she herself did. She praised Uttam, then told Sarbani to hold on to her good man, for she had got herself a great *find*! She yawned when Uttam and Sarbani sat down to watch *E.T. the Extra-Terrestrial* during a random channel change, and said that she had watched it when she was 'oh so young!'.

Uttam said, 'So were we,' and drew Sarbani close. He then got up to insert a hard drive into the TV and put on Pink Floyd.

Ritu looked surprised.

'Takes us straight back to our college days,' said Uttam.

'Yeah, because schooldays was for ABBA,' Sarbani giggled.

'Oh, I still enjoy ABBA,' said Ritu sipping her Bloody Mary.

'So do we,' Sarbani replied.

Uttam handed her a glass with two fingers of Jameson in it. He raised his own glass. 'To the '70s! When we were young and romantic.'

But before Sarbani could respond, Ritu launched into a long story about how naïve she was when they had met.

'Do you remember?' she said turning eagerly towards Sarbani. 'That day when we thought we'd bunk class and took a bus to Esplanade?'

Sarbani thought she should tell her that she wasn't part of that escapade as she was a boarder then, but changed her mind.

After she left, Sarbani called her once to find out if she'd had a safe flight, and Ritu kept saying that both of them had gone out of their way, beyond the call of duty, for her. Then, almost six months later, she emailed her complaining that she had never understood why Sarbani had turned cold, etc. etc. Two months later, Sarbani, suddenly feeling sentimental, called her on Skype. But Ritu cut her short saying she was busy. The next time she visited India, she emailed Sarbani about her impending journey, but didn't contact her after landing. And the year after that, Sarbani didn't tell her she was relocating to the US since Uttam was being 'kicked upstairs' as he liked to put it.

FERAL

A 45-degree slope led the way to Maya Kaikobad's quarters. Moushumi climbed slowly; she wasn't used to hilly places. Ahead, Satwaki walked briskly, holding Mimi's hand. Mimi, in turn, held Rishi's hand, forming a frisky, curly-haired link between the father and son. The breeze had begun to turn chilly as the sun cooled to a burnt brick shade, growing moodier by the minute. Everything looked as if it had been painted in the colours artists would choose if they picturized poems.

Moushumi jogged her mind, but failed to remember the poet's name, the one who made her think of painters visualizing poems on canvas or paper. A few lines drifted in and out of her head, ruffling her thoughts, just like the evening breeze. She remembered 'Daffodils' from her middle-school days, and now a few lines from that poem fluttered in her mind like the petals of those very flowers in a meadow. Funny, she mused, how Indian grass grew in fields, but those in England were always in meadows! The school they had come to in the Nilgiris reminded her of these things, English things, she'd read about. Its old Victorian buildings, orderly flower beds, large pedigree dogs and teachers' cottages tucked behind a sudden copse of eucalyptus and other tall trees took Moushumi away to a land she was familiar with only in books. A woman's low laugh brought her back to her surroundings.

They were here to get Rishi admitted. The school was old and prestigious, and both Satwaki and Moushumi had heaved a collective sigh of relief when they had received the confirmation letter. They had arrived three days ahead of Rishi's admission date, and like any other tourist family, had gone sightseeing and picnicking in and around Coonoor and Ooty. Moushumi had already shopped for extra warm clothes and thermal underwear for Rishi in Singapore, but she still wanted to check out Ooty's markets. The school provided uniforms and sundry warm clothes and blankets, but Moushumi hadn't liked them. The colours were dull and the material scratchy.

'Considering the steep school fees, you'd think they'd provide better quality!' she grumbled to Satwaki.

He said nothing. He didn't want to come across as a pinchpenny. A nice bright cotton slipcover would have solved both problems as far as he was concerned, why buy expensive stuff? Things got stolen or lost in boarding schools.

They had reached the school premises earlier in the day, nervous and much ahead of schedule. They had met most of the teachers and the headmaster during tea, a dainty spread of mostly confectioneries and savoury puffs baked by the school's own bakery, and tea and coffee served in plain white cups and saucers with the school's insignia. This was a school ritual for all new students, more than a century old. There were other parents with their children sitting at the tables laid out in the lawn. All were new students, though some had older siblings already in the school, and many of the parents were alumni. Both Satwaki and Moushumi noticed the difference between the parents who were ex-students and those who were not straightaway. There was an invisible barrier between them, which came through in the way the parents carried themselves and how the school teachers and staff treated them. They were on sure ground, familiar territory. They spoke with confidence with the teachers, their acquaintances and friends. They ignored the other parents, not necessarily out of rudeness, but because they didn't notice them at all. They were the insiders.

Putting Rishi in a boarding school, one with a history, or 'pedigree' as Satwaki's father used to say, had been a dream for both him and Moushumi, neither of whom had had that experience. Satwaki had gone to various schools, wherever his father had been posted—schools that the children of most army officers attended. He had finished his schooling at St Xavier's school though, when his father was posted in Kolkata. Moushumi, born and raised in Kolkata, had been to a typical old Kolkata institution, an academically sound, but semi-English-medium school, with more stress on Bengali than spoken English. She spoke English fluently, but with a marked Bengali accent.

Satwaki was doing well in his career. He had recently been transferred to Singapore as head of his company's operations. Satwaki often spoke of the school alumni groups some of his colleagues and business associates belonged to.

'It's like a club,' he'd told her. 'That's a clique my son should be able to relate to.'

Moushumi had never stayed away from Rishi even for a single night. But she kept her feelings to herself. It was for the good of the child. They were not trying to shirk their parental responsibilities. She knew how Satwaki felt during some of the office get-togethers. Not that she felt any better. What was it about schools that set people apart no matter how well they did in life later on, including degrees from prestigious institutes? Moushumi shook her head at the thought as she climbed up the incline leading to the junior boys' hostel and beyond.

They had taken the first step for their children. Rishi had been admitted. A few years later, Mimi would join him. Their children would be part of a luminous alumni. As if he'd read her thoughts, Satwaki looked back and smiled.

The breeze blew her hair and Satwaki motioned her to stop as he took a shot with his camera. He seemed a lot more relaxed now that all the formalities were over and they were free to explore the substantial grounds and chat with any teacher who happened to be available.

'Hurry, Ma!' said Mimi and immediately turned back to skip alongside her brother. Mimi was even more excited than Rishi about his school. She had already made plans about which horse she would ride and on which side of the long dining hall she would sit. Rishi smiled when she announced her preferences.

'You don't choose your seat,' he said. 'They *allot* you one.'

Mimi didn't know the meaning of the word 'allot' so she stuck her tongue out at Rishi. But he continued to smile indulgently. Satwaki and Moushumi were certain he would be able to work his way around and later shine in the school. Rishi had always been at the top of his class. He also seemed to instinctively know what was expected of him, and tried to fulfil his parents' expectations without fuss. When it came to Mimi, he was very avuncular and that suited the girl just fine, because she never lost any opportunity to take advantage of Rishi.

Now the two of them continued ahead, walking-skipping, hands linked, along the path with pretty wild flowers growing in clumps on both sides, their father having long given up his hold on the energetic Mimi. The evening settled around the children, creating a pale silvery halo. Moushumi had a sudden urge to sit on one of the smoothed-down boulders and weep. By now they had reached a fork in the path. The narrower one with cypress hedges almost hiding it from view, led the way to Maya Kaikobad's house.

Maya had kept the door ajar, so she could see them coming before they reached her gate. Her cottage was a little away from the rest of the teachers' homes. The ground, covered with thick green grass and wild flowers, fell steeply away right behind her house, giving it a suspended-in-the-air kind of look. She didn't care for gardening so the lack of extra ground didn't bother her. If anything, she enjoyed the solitude, the space between hers and theirs, and the emptiness behind. Thomas sat licking his paws near the door that was left ajar, where a bar of retreating sunlight warmed his twitching tail.

'Meow,' said Thomas at the sound of Mimi's voice.

'Yes. Let them in, Thomas,' said Maya. 'New student's parents need attention,' she muttered as she walked back to the kitchen. She struck a match to the gas stove. She couldn't remember what the mother looked like, even though they'd met that morning. Maya recalled the mother, the faceless and nameless mother, eager to please, eager to see her son learn the piano, the violin and singing! The woman seemed eager for everything. 'Upstarts!'

A shriek brought Maya quickly to the front door. Mimi stood with a shocked expression on her face, holding up her index finger. Thomas was nowhere to be seen. Moushumi was furiously rummaging through the depths of her copious handbag.

'Your cat bit me,' said Mimi matter-of-factly. 'What's her name?'

'Thomas. He's a tomcat,' said Maya, almost smiling. 'Bleeding?'

'Thomas is a boy cat,' Mimi announced to no one in particular. 'No blood. See? I'm strong.'

'Come in. Come in,' said Maya stepping back into her parlour.

Satwaki and Rishi entered and muttered their greetings. Satwaki sat down on the nearest sofa. Moushumi had unearthed a packet of band-aids. She knelt down to attend to Mimi's finger.

'Oh. So, you're one of those moms,' said Maya.

'Is your cat even vaccinated?' asked Moushumi. She didn't sound eager-to-please at all. Her large eyes flashed in the darkening evening.

Maya frowned. She turned towards Satwaki. 'Which country did you say?'

'Singapore.'

'That's not too far. We have children from the UK and even Canada. One child, parents divorced. The mother's in Canada, but the grandparents stay in Kochi.'

'Which class is the child in?' said Satwaki.

'Class VIII.'

'Look at my finger,' said Mimi and bounded across to Rishi who stood respectfully near a wall in Maya's parlour.

'What did you say your name was, boy?' said Maya. 'Sit down. Sit down,' she waved her hands. 'Make yourselves comfy.'

'Rishi, ma'am.'

'Which class? XI?'

'No five,' said Moushumi brusquely. 'He'll turn ten this November. He's a little young for his class. And ahead,' but the last bit she muttered only to herself.

'I'm five,' said Mimi. 'My birthday's in September. Na, baba?' She made herself comfortable on Satwaki's lap. 'Aunty, where's Thomas, the tomcat?'

'Go to the garden and see if he's there, chasing sparrows or mice. He was such a feral thing when I found him. Still a bit wild. Though vastly improved now.'

'Mimi, be careful, sweetheart,' said Moushumi. She got up and followed Mimi to the door.

'Oh, don't worry,' said Maya, before shrugging irritably and turning to Rishi. 'Can you play?'

Rishi who had been listening to her attentively, nodded, and smiled shyly.

'He had a teacher in Singapore. But he's just started,' said Satwaki.

'Play me something,' said Maya.

Rishi looked up at his father. Satwaki gave him a little push.

'It's all right,' said Satwaki in a low voice. 'This is not a test. Just play.'

Rishi walked gingerly towards the black upright piano at the corner of the parlour. He looked at the piano and then at his parents.

'Play,' mouthed Moushumi from the door.

'I'll get you folks some coffee. Hot chocolate for the children?' said Maya.

'Yes, thank you,' said Satwaki.

'Mimi, aunty's getting hot chocolate for you. Come in,' said Moushumi.

'Play, Rishi,' said Satwaki.

Rishi lifted the lid and the velvet cloth that covered the keys. He sat down on the piano stool, and ran his fingers over the keys, east to west and west to east, paused and looked around once before resting his fingers on the centre keys. Rishi closed his eyes for a few seconds in concentration and then began to play. He didn't look up during the time he played, six pieces in all. Behind him, his parents sat listening, nervous on his behalf. Maya watched them, first the boy, the mother and then the father. Mimi was the only one who was unaffected by the atmosphere. She had managed to become friends with Thomas, and was stroking him and murmuring endearments. Thomas seemed to enjoy her attention and had completely forgotten about his earlier hostility.

'How long have you been learning?' said Maya when Rishi finished.

'One-and-a-half years,' said Moushumi.

'Let him say, Mou,' said Satwaki, adding almost immediately, 'I think one year, and seven-and-a-half months.'

Rishi nodded and looked at Maya expectantly.

'You'll improve,' she said. 'Is the sugar okay in your coffee? And, you, Miss Muffet? Your hot chocolate, okay?'

'I'm letting it cool first,' said Mimi, swinging her legs.

Thomas got down from her lap. Mimi got up.

'No,' said Moushumi. 'Drink your chocolate first.'

Mimi grinned at Maya. Maya tweaked her nose and walked across the room, to an armchair near the sofa where Satwaki was sitting.

'You know, I'm half-Burmese,' she said, crossing and uncrossing her legs, and then crossing them again. 'Half from my mother's side. My parents got divorced when I was four. I stayed with my dad and his family. I've lived on almost every continent in the world.'

Moushumi quickly left her armchair and sat down next to Satwaki. 'That must have been many years ago, right?' she said.

'In those days, divorce wasn't common, was it?' said Satwaki.

'Those days were in 1960,' said Maya uncrossing her long legs. 'We were so erudite!' She laughed, somewhat mirthlessly.

'Oh,' said Moushumi, and very softly under her breath, savouring the new word, she murmured, 'erudite'.

'I attended a finishing school in Switzerland. But my heart was in music, so I went to Germany after that. You know, I've been with the Calcutta Choir since its inception, almost. They've renamed the city Kolkata!' She waved a dismissive hand even though her audience showed no disagreement. 'Pish posh! It was made by the British.'

'Your husband is also into music?' said Moushumi.

'I don't have a husband. Not now.'

'Oh?' said Satwaki and Moushumi together.

'I came to this school to drill some music sense into the kids. And also, for the air. Hills, you know.'

'Yes,' said Satwaki. 'Purer. Indian cities are so polluted.'

'But hill stations have become so touristy these days. I'm not sure I can stand it any more. And then the quality of people. In my time, you had to come from a certain kind of family to get admission into a boarding school like this . . .'

'I know what you mean,' said Satwaki. 'My father was in the army. He felt the same way about civilians.'

'Oh, you have an army background? So, what was your father?'

'He was a doctor.'

'Oh? A doctor?' She fluttered her fingers. 'Don't mind me,' she said airily. 'I'm just an old romantic. You know soldiers and men in uniforms . . .' Maya turned towards Moushumi. 'And your father?'

'Both my parents were professors at Calcutta University.'

'Ah yes,' said Maya. 'That unmistakable accent. I've lived in Cal for, how many years? More than twenty–thirty, now.' She turned towards Rishi, 'And what do you want to be when you grow up?'

'I want to be a deep-sea diver,' said Mimi.

Rishi smiled.

'Good for you!' said Maya. 'Rishi, you have a sweet smile. Now, I'll play you a couple of pieces, okay?'

Rishi nodded, still shy but pleased. Mimi went up and leaned against Rishi. 'Play for me too,' she said to Maya. Satwaki leaned forward.

'It's getting late,' said Moushumi. But nobody paid her any attention.

Maya played elegantly, her body swaying with the music. She played an easy piece by Tchaikovsky first, and then quickly moved on to Mozart's Piano Concerto No. 21. She followed it up with Beethoven's Symphony No. 9. When she began to play Mozart's Symphony No. 40 in G minor, Molto Allegro, Satwaki and Moushumi looked at each other. They smiled in mutual recognition of the music. It was one their favourite Hindi film songs. They hadn't known about its classical origins! The idea delighted them. They continued to smile throughout the piece, but without comprehension, except when the first familiar bars were repeated.

'Recognize this?' said Maya when she began playing Beethoven's Symphony No. 5 in C minor.

Satwaki grinned. 'Saturday Night Fever!'

Maya turned her head to smile at him and continued playing. She ended her performance with a nocturne by Chopin. Mimi, who had slowly crept forward with each new piece that was played, now stood at Maya's shoulder, almost breathing on her arm.

'Aunty, you play like a queen. A real fairy queen!' whispered Mimi in an enraptured voice the minute Maya finished.

'Really?' said Maya. She ran a playful finger all the way from Mimi's curls to her chin. 'And you look like a little elf yourself. Dancing in the moonlight.'

Maya rose from the piano seat, a faint smile playing on her lips, but her eyes seemed to have drawn in the dulcet yet contemplative notes from the nocturne. Her shadow elongated against the wall with regal grace. Satwaki and Moushumi also rose, as if to remain seated would have been a violation of the evening. Rishi seemed transfixed and had to be pulled to his feet by Mimi. Maya saw them to the door and raising a hand, she fluttered two fingers. Satwaki ducked his head. Mimi waved her hand like a flag. Rishi said, 'Bye, ma'am,' but so softly nobody heard. Moushumi barely nodded in acknowledgement, and strode ahead, her hand on Rishi's shoulder.

Later, when the three of them walked back to the school guard house, beyond which their taxi waited, Mimi almost dragged her feet, and was unusually quiet. She hadn't cried when they had said goodbye to Rishi in front of his dormitory, under the kindly but firm eyes of the housemaster. They had watched as Rishi had gathered his almost ten-year-old dignity around his shoulders like a cloak and walked down the long corridor, never once glancing back. Mimi had caught hold of her parents' hands, one in each of her own, and had pulled them away with all her strength when Rishi's back had finally disappeared around a bend. They were silent, almost still, throughout the ride back to their hotel. The three of them felt claustrophobic in their hotel room, so summoning the hotel's taxi service, they set out to eat elsewhere, a nice restaurant that served alcohol, preferably.

Moushumi, Satwaki and Mimi ended up weeping simultaneously during dinner, after they had 'cheered', Satwaki raising his whiskey glass, Moushumi her gin and lime and Mimi her vanilla chocolate float. They didn't care who watched them. The tears just came, turning their drinks salty. They couldn't eat, but Moushumi, ever the frugal mother, asked for the uneaten portions to be boxed. Satwaki didn't protest that it would be wasted since they were going to return to their hotel, not home. He was too overcome by emotion to bother. They took the overnight train to Chennai the next day, and the flight back to Singapore the same night, after freshening up and eating lunch at a hotel near the airport.

During the days that followed, after their return, Mimi diligently checked the letter box downstairs on her way back from school. At Rishi's school, they were encouraged to write letters on paper, not email, though the school administration and teachers kept parents abreast of everything through their website and individual emails. A letter arrived at last, after weeks of waiting, and it was fat with news. Satwaki hurried home from office after Mimi's excited phone call. She hadn't opened the letter, nor had she allowed Moushumi to do so. The two of them watched excitedly, like children beneath a Christmas tree, as Satwaki did the honours. Rishi had written a separate letter to each of them. Some details overlapped, like the school routine and new friends that Rishi had made. But there was something exclusive for each of them.

Mimi's letter carried many doodles and sketches and descriptions of the horses and their names. Satwaki's letter contained Rishi's study plans and details about the teachers. To Moushumi, he wrote about Maya and Thomas:

Dearest Ma,

Maya Ma'am didn't stay. She left a couple of weeks after we met her, when she had played like a fairy queen, like Mimi said! Thomas didn't go with her. He has become a feral cat now. Yesterday I saw him and called. I had a biscuit in my hand, but he only looked at me suspiciously and ran off. I heard something about Maya Ma'am. People are saying that she packed the piano along with

her furniture. The piano belonged to the school. I don't
know how true this is . . .

Moushumi read the letter to herself again after she'd read
it out to Mimi and Satwaki. This was to become the first of
a family ritual, the opening of Rishi's letter together and
reading each portion to each other. That day, she also took
Rishi's letter to a corner and reread it for the umpteenth
time from the first word to the last, slowly. When she
came across the portion about Maya Kaikobad, she smiled
grimly, but her tongue caressed the word 'feral' in her
mouth, over and over again. 'My clever boy,' she said to
herself, 'he heard it just once and already knows it, and can
even use it in a sentence!'

GUAVA

'Ram Singh!' shrieked Mrs Bhaduri. 'Ram Singh!'

The boys swung from the branches of the guava tree like monkeys. Mrs Bhaduri advanced. They ignored her and continued to plunder the tree. She picked up a slender bamboo pole with an iron hook attached. The hooked end of the pole was used to twist and break off the stems of the out-of-reach guavas. Mrs Bhaduri brandished it like a lance.

To the thin and diminutive child watching the drama from a safe distance, the pole in her mother's hand reminded her of Captain Hook's arm. She had heard the story from Rima, her elder sister. Rahul, her older brother, was two years her senior and a year younger than Rima. But he was the scion, and therefore, the baby of the family for all practical purposes. He never told her any stories. He preferred beating her up on the flimsiest of excuses. Their mother never reprimanded him. As for their father, he noticed little when he was sober, and even less when he was drunk.

A hush had descended among the tatterdemalions. Each one of them eyed the pole warily from his perch on the tree. Those lower down arched their bare feet, ready to jump off the second the iron hook came within an inch of their skins.

The girl wondered why the boys' uniforms were shabby. And why they wore torn sandals and cheap plastic flip-flops or were completely barefoot instead of wearing socks and shoes. Rima and Rahul wore crisp white uniforms and blue silk ties to school. Their black Bata shoes were always polished to a shine. They had white canvas shoes, Keds, for the games period, and these they carried separately in jute bags. Their books and lunch boxes filled their satchels. She wanted to go to school too. She would turn five a few months later. But her father was oblivious and her mother scoffed at her, saying that she had to wait and be a good girl while she was at it or else there wouldn't be any school at all.

She knew the boys hated her siblings. She had seen them lobbing hard inedible guavas at Rahul and Rima a few times. Once they had even broken a window pane in their bedroom. So far, they hadn't tried to harm her.

Now as she watched her mother's face turn bright with anger, her eyes involuntarily widened. With the long pole in her hand and her long black hair and sari flowing around her pale buxom body, Mrs Bhaduri looked like Ma Durga about to slay the demons. The pole had never nicked any thieving limb so far. Nevertheless, bright button eyes looked down suspiciously at the woman and the child. A grim stillness descended over the garden. It seemed to the girl that even the crows and parrots lurking among the foliage were awaiting her mother's next move.

'If you filthy urchins don't come down this instant!' said Mrs Bhaduri, brandishing her pole, 'I will not only set Ram Singh on you, but the dogs as well!'

From behind the hedges a man laughed, the sound low against the rustle of guava leaves. A boy dangling closest to Mrs Bhaduri's weapon jumped off with a whoop, and the rest, as if on cue, followed. Leaves and twigs fluttered down. A few guavas rolled out from their pockets during the mad scramble to escape. Scrawny brown arms and legs untangled on the tarmac on the other side of the hedge. Hastily flung down satchels were slung back on shoulders with equal haste. The boys departed, yelling rude comments. Mrs Bhaduri's gaze remained immaculately disdainful. She sailed back into the house as soon as they had left.

There was, in truth, no Ram Singh. As for the dogs, there was only one left now, a mutt that was too old to even snap at the fleas on his mangy coat. The only other pet left was a freeloading cat and her kittens.

Mrs Bhaduri mentioned Ram Singh's name with confidence. As if he could be conjured from the distant past of her childhood. She was the daughter of a Rai Bahadur who used to hobnob with white British officers and businessmen and employed Anglo-Indian ladies to teach English and table manners to the women in his family. Now twenty years after Independence, there were no more phaetons and Austin cars. The mansion with its two marble lions flanking the stairs had been sold off. She had been married off to a man who had a job as a manager at a coal mine, which he retained thanks to the goodwill of the owners who had known his father, the scion of an ancient if slightly murky zamindari family. Still, Mrs Bhaduri was a kulin brahmin. She had the high forehead and straight nose of her ancestors. If she cried out for Ram Singh, whether he existed or not, you were expected to believe her.

Mrs Bhaduri ordered the girl to run her fingers through her hair as she returned to her interrupted siesta. The child did as she was told. She was not strong enough to rebel openly. Her brother and sister escaped the daily afternoon torture by answering back and running away before their irate mother could catch and thrash them. After ten minutes, Mrs Bhaduri started to snore delicately through her translucent nostrils, her peach-coloured lips slightly parted. The child gingerly lifted her fingers from her mother's hair and tiptoed away to her dolls.

The boys did not return that afternoon. The children had the garden to themselves. Rima and Rahul clambered up the largest trees; mango, jackfruit, jamun and the prince of their garden—the guava tree. The girl, now tired of playing 'house–house' with only her dolls for company, wandered around with the ring and middle fingers of her right hand inside her mouth and a kitten in her left. She looked up. Her siblings were effortlessly negotiating the branches. She wondered when she would be big enough to climb so high.

The girl went to the rear part of the compound, the less frequented part. It had some trees and bushes. A deep, wide drain, rich with slime, ran through it. She imagined it to be a moat in which a dark, scaly and smelly beast lurked. The trees were either thorny or too thin. And there wasn't enough bare ground to run around in. The place had an eerie, forlorn aura about it. Rima and Rahul avoided coming here. She did too, but lately she had been feeling utterly squeezed out from all the possible spaces at home. It distressed her. Worse, she couldn't understand the reasons. And that made her feel breathless, and constantly seek escape.

The old gardener who had stayed on because he was too old to go anywhere else, came here to smoke his bidis. He sat on his haunches near the drain, dragging on his smoke and coughing up gobs of phlegm. There was a brass tap above a cement slab, which covered a small portion of the drain. The gardener fixed a long hose pipe to it whenever he watered the entire garden and the tiny holes in the pipe created mini fountains all the way to the vegetable patches and flower beds.

The gardener was absent, but the hose pipe was still attached to the tap. The girl decided to open the tap. She put the kitten down, a safe distance away from the tap. Superfine jets of water hit her face and arms through tiny punctures in the pipe. She jumped with delight. Her frock was soon wet, but she didn't care. After a while she grew tired of the water game, and wandered off again.

A squirrel caught her attention. She chased it to the edge, and stopped short. For there, growing almost into the hedge, was a slender guava tree, a mere stripling of a tree, barely six feet tall. She looked at it curiously. Its branches were so low that she could jump up and pull them down. It was too thin to climb. She tried and found she could bend the trunk until it touched her shoulders. She pulled the two lowest branches around her. The fresh, slightly piquant fragrance of the guava leaves filled her lungs. Through the parting she saw a guava. A single fruit, almost oval, glistening green like a huge jade. Her mother had a jade ring set in silver with intricate designs encircling the cool dark smoothness of the pigeon-egg sized stone. She thought it was the most beautiful ring in the world, a magical thing, and had dared to ask about it. Her mother had responded curtly. Her siblings called her a greedy pig who would grow up to be a jewel thief. Her mother had done nothing to stop the name calling. The girl decided to keep her guava a secret.

Apart from the near-ripe guava, there was something else that intrigued her. The tree's peeling bark. Barks of guava trees peeled easily, but this was such a young tree. Besides, it was not so much the peeling bark, but the patterns it had made. The tree seemed to be full of faces. One in particular, low enough to be at eye level, looked like an old man's face. A smiling and kindly face, and when the breeze made the tree sway, the face seemed to nod at her and smile like the grandfather she still remembered, though dimly.

She thought it was grand that she had found a playmate, even if he was just a tree bark face. She hoped the face would be there again the next day. To her delight it was. Clearer than the day before. She felt she could talk to her old-man-in-a-bark friend, and watch her precious guava grow at the same time.

The girl took to hurrying to the rear garden in the afternoons. Once there, she began telling her new friend the day's news, no matter how trivial. One day to her surprise, he actually replied, softly, so no one could hear except her. His lips did not appear to move, and his voice seemed to come from the hedge, which shielded the garden from a narrow and little used public path behind the house.

Loneliness overruled fear, the natural defence mechanism of all small creatures. The joy of finding someone or something that responded to her without mockery and spite, buried any suspicion, the first reaction of the downtrodden towards any act of sudden kindness. It did not take her long to start exchanging confidences along with her girlish gossip. She told her friend how angry her mother was at her for not being born a boy. He replied by calling her his fairy princess.

A few days later, the girl heard her mother screaming again. This time the old gardener stood nearby, holding the pole. He shoved its hook end into the branches from time to time like a bayonet. A boy's foot scraped against the hook. There was a howl of protest. The boys dropped from the tree, cursing and abusing. The language they used set Mrs Bhaduri's ears aflame. But she stood her ground. She had good reason to be extra vigilant. There would be another get-together of the ladies' club, which meant preparing tiffin for the members, with each assigned member vying to show off her culinary skills.

Mrs Bhaduri's guava jelly and guava cheese were famous, especially the cheese. She believed they owed their taste and texture to her tree's bounty, but of course would never admit so in public. You never knew which jealous soul would have the tree cut down, perhaps even killed with witchcraft and devilish concoctions in the dead of night. Her ladies' club friends were not above it. They were in fact not above anything, even husband stealing. Mrs Bhaduri almost snorted at the thought. Nobody would steal Mr Bhaduri though. And she, herself, was too blue-blooded to belong to anyone other than the man with whom she had walked seven times around the fire to seal her marriage. She had seen how her friends' husbands looked at her. Quick, furtive. Tinged with lust. But nobody would dare approach her, she knew. She was above them all.

Mrs Bhaduri watched the gardener tear down the ripest fruits with the hook. When he had managed to pluck enough, he bent down to collect them, and in the process also those that had fallen before, half eaten by bats and birds. She appeared not to notice, and waited only until the plastic basket was full before withdrawing into the house.

The three children followed, already anticipating the guava jelly, which would be later smeared over tiny fresh-from-the-bakery buns and thin slices of home-baked sponge cake. There would be clotted cream and cubes of red guava cheese served in their individual cut glass bowls. But these were not for them. They would get some jelly on plain bread and butter. Only after their mother's friends had had their fill, would they get to taste the cheese, buns and cake. Mrs Bhaduri was never one to skimp on food, except when the times were hard.

The little girl soon slipped away to look at her secret guava and talk to her secret friend. The guava had grown larger since. Her friend said she should stand on tippy toes and smell it. She did. The sharp astringent scent delighted her.

'When do you think I can eat it?' she asked.

'Oh, it's ripe enough. I can already taste it,' he replied, adding, 'the best things in life are worth waiting for.' And, laughed coarsely.

It shocked her, and made the hairs stand up on her arms. Something was not right. She stood there confused, unsure whether to run off or ignore the feeling. The sky meanwhile had turned lurid with orange streaks cutting through the clouds. It was still too early for the birds to return. This was the hour when grown-ups stretched a little more to prolong their siestas; school-going children rushed through their homework so they could have the rest of the evening free. Something stirred in her mind, a tiny warning bell. She turned, poised on her toes, ready to flee.

Nobody noticed her absence until late at night. Mrs Bhaduri was particularly annoyed. Her guests were arriving the next day for afternoon tea. She had been hard at work all day so dinner was Govind Bhog rice with boiled potatoes and ghee. She wouldn't compromise on the rice, no matter what. There was no cook to take on the drudgery part of cooking. So, when Mrs Bhaduri had to make special dishes, their everyday meals tended to be basic.

'She's done it before, the little rascal,' muttered Mrs Bhaduri. She decided to ignore the absence until after the party. Where would the brat go anyway, except to the empty servants' quarters? Let her stay there hungry and dirty. Serve her right!

Rima and Rahul didn't miss her until the next afternoon, when the excitement of the special tiffin made them forget their habitual contempt for her. They yelled for her to come out, threatening to eat her share. When she didn't reply, they asked the old gardener.

'Chhoti baba has been playing at the back,' he said pulling on his bidi. He didn't bother to get up. He had run many errands for madam, and now felt he deserved to sit and smoke in peace.

The two children left him and went in search. Their initial annoyance had now turned into missionary zeal. They had to find her, if only to teach her a lesson for disappearing. They discovered the guava, tantalizingly luscious. It dangled several inches above them, so they pulled the branch down and plucked the fruit. It was delicious. The best guava they'd ever shared. The face was there as well, a little askew, but still discernible, if one were to go looking for faces in tree barks. Rima and Rahul didn't see it. They saw something else.

Their little sister's knickers, muddied and a bit torn, lying near the drain. They found one of her slippers too, face down, like her, when she cried by herself on the bed. They stood there puzzling over it for a while. But instinct told them that the torn knickers was taboo. Perhaps the biggest taboo of all things to tell their mother. They decided to keep quiet by mutual and unspoken consent, and let the grown-ups do the discovering. They returned to the prospect of buns and jelly with renewed determination. It didn't take them long to forget all about the knickers and their missing sister.

Mrs Bhaduri was momentarily embarrassed when one of her guests asked about her third child. She managed to brush the harmless question away with a remark about dolls. Her older children were a joy to behold in their neat clothes and smart manners. Afterwards, she quizzed the gardener. When he failed to give her a satisfactory answer, a search party was launched comprising herself, her sober-for-a-change husband and the gardener. They found the slipper first. The police had to be informed after they found the knickers.

It was the kind of scandal that evokes pity and solicitousness, however unwanted. Mrs Bhaduri, unsurprisingly, handled the situation with grace and stoicism. Afterwards, she took to chaperoning Rima everywhere, under the sympathetic approval of the townsfolk. Rahul was sent away to a residential school. No photographs of the disappeared child hung from any wall or stood propped up on any table. Her name was never mentioned. And soon it was as if she had never been named at all. The small guava tree bore nothing after that one luscious fruit. The big guava tree remained loyally bountiful, but its tormentors never returned. As for Rima and Rahul, they soon lost interest in the tree.

WHAT LINGERS

'The real reason for getting close to another woman is hate. You must really hate her,' said Nayanika as she arranged dried flowers in a rattan basket.

I shifted uncomfortably. I had come to share something with her before we left Singapore for good. 'What's that supposed to mean?' I said, after a pause.

Nayanika laughed. 'Vani dear. Look at all of us here. Our circle of frogs in the expat well.'

I stirred my tea without enthusiasm. I like my tea thick with milk, very sweet and redolent of cardamom. But according to Nayanika, tea must be steeped in a porcelain teapot before being poured into porcelain cups. The milk in its little jug and the sugar in its bowl placed on a tray along with the tea. According to me her method is a waste of time. Her tea is thin and bland. I boil my decoction—milk, tea, water, cardamom pods and sugar—in a saucepan.

The others in our group drink my kind of tea, except when they are with Nayanika.

I'd first met Nayanika at a typical Indian birthday party, where the mothers are dressed to kill and the food is a mish-mash of Singaporean and Indian—vegetarian bee hoon, samosas, *heeng* kachoris and chutney, vegetable fried rice, vegetable dumplings or spring rolls, two varieties of soft drinks, cake and ice cream. A party organizer kept the children occupied, while the mothers got acquainted and re-acquainted, eyeing each other's jewellery, discussing holiday plans, the children's grades and how bad a particular teacher was. They tried subtle ways to find out whose husband was earning more, who was shifting to a bigger condominium and so on. In between, they tossed the latest about their respective in-laws and gossiped about an absentee member of the group.

I'd once mentioned to Viren, my husband, that we should move to a better house. But he was firm. Two recessions had already hit Singapore and job conditions were shaky. He'd rather be on firmer ground moneywise before we start acting rich. I know he's right. And, honestly speaking, the only time I feel bad is right after such gatherings, when I've listened to the women. I become silent as I go about my housework. The old Hindi film numbers that I usually hum stay stuck in my throat, until the lump becomes too big and I have to shed the tears. If I can't stop the tears, I go to the bathroom. But once it happened while I was scrubbing our steel pots at the sink. Viren caught me sniffling. He came really close, but couldn't say or do anything because his sister came into the kitchen just then. Later on, when we were alone, Viren stroked my hair quietly and held me close. He didn't say anything. He didn't have to.

Viren's sister, Nita, also stays with us. She was married before, but that didn't work out, and she returned home. Viren brought her to Singapore so the family could avoid gossipy relatives and neighbours, and his parents could spend their old age in peace. Nita has some qualifications in computers. She is smart too. Viren was able to get her a job soon. The plan was that Nita would work and save her salary till another suitable and broadminded groom was found for her. Except that things are hardly as simple. Nayanika knows about my problems. She's always lent a sympathetic ear whenever I needed to let out steam.

'Is it true then, that you're leaving Singapore?' said Nayanika, taking my untouched cup away.

I stared at her, open mouthed. 'How did you know?'

'Small community. Word gets around.'

'Then you also know why I'm leaving!'

'Something about Nita, right?'

'You have all the gossip,' I said bitterly.

Ignoring me, she said, 'Why did you indulge Savita?'

I didn't understand what she meant.

'Look,' she said. 'I won't beat about the bush. Savita cottoned on to me right after your marathon phone session with her. But instead of her learning anything new, I learnt about Nita!'

'Is that why you mentioned staying close to the one you hate?'

'Well, it was on my mind . . . Viren earns more than her husband. She's bound to resent that.'

'Nita was caught shoplifting,' I blurted out the words, and nearly gagged in the process.

She looked at me for few seconds. 'I'll boil you some tea. You're going to have to drink all of it!' she said trying to look severe.

I got up from the couch and followed her. We sat opposite each other at her kitchen table. She pushed a mug of steaming tea towards me. 'There's more,' she said.

I took a sip. 'You boiled the tea?'

'Desperate times need desperate measures,' she said. Her eyes held compassion, even as her lips smiled.

'It happened at Mustafa Centre,' I said after a few more sips. 'We'd gone there to buy presents. Viren's cousin is getting married back home.' I paused. I took a long swig from my mug, and held the tea in my mouth for a few seconds before swallowing. 'They caught her at the exit. She had a perfume bottle in her bag.'

I drained my mug. Nayanika refilled it. Her long slim fingers lightly touched mine.

'She stole a perfume bottle! Imagine that?! They called the police. Sent her to jail. She was there the whole night.

Viren had to enlist his boss' help to stand security. And, now she's got that stamp of conviction or whatever it is they call it here . . . Oh, Nika, we've lost face. She can't work here any more. She has to return to India. We can't stay here any more. The whole thing is so shameful. Viren cried last night, you know. How I hate Nita!'

'Vani, Singapore has strict laws. Personal integrity means a lot here. Now the laws may seem unduly harsh to you. But in a small country like Singapore, it makes sense. But why are you two leaving? Let Nita go.'

'Viren's lost face in his office, Nika. You know how he is. He won't stay. He's already asked for a transfer. Lucky for us, there is a place vacant in Bangalore. And to think her second marriage is already fixed!'

'Viren's made up his mind?'

'We are leaving Singapore in three weeks!' I felt the tears rising again. 'Why did she have to be so greedy?! She's spoilt everything for me! We were so happy here!'

'Hmm,' said Nayanika, and looked at me intently.

'I enjoyed being far away from the rest of my in-laws. At least here I only had to put up with them for two or three months at the most each year. Back home, I'll be literally living with them. Viren and I had become quite close here, you know. He even used to help me with the housework at times.'

She patted my hand. I wiped my face with a tissue that she handed me. 'We had just begun to settle down and I was looking forward to going somewhere else next summer, instead of India. We planned to buy so many things. Now there's no time and not enough money. Viren had a target, you know, about how much we would make here.'

'You should be able to pick up a few things, nice things within these few weeks.'

'Like what?' I said. 'It doesn't make sense buying electronic items because for starters they are all available in India nowadays, well mostly. And who's going to get it serviced if there's a glitch? As for clothes, I anyway wear salwar suits and saris in India. Nika, I wanted to go places, pick up souvenirs, you know. Everyone goes here and there. Then they come back with things and photos. I mean, look at your house; it's full of stuff you've picked up from all over the world. Another year or so and we too would be travelling, just like you.'

My words sounded petty and childish even to my own ears. But Nayanika didn't look contemptuous. If anything, she looked concerned.

'I've travelled a bit, could have travelled more. But tell me, Vani, would it have made you a happier person if you could've filled up your house with things brought from holiday destinations?'

'Well, it's nice to be well-travelled, own nice things and all. You don't have to say it, people would see, and know straightaway.'

'You don't have to travel to pick up souvenirs. If you know where to shop.'

I didn't know what she meant. 'I know you can get most things right here in Singapore. But what about those two four-feet-high carved wooden elephants, you got them from Cambodia, didn't you?' I said. 'And, those big wooden Jazz players? Aren't they from the US?'

Nayanika smiled.

'I think you still have time to shop for such things,' she paused. 'I love thrift stores and pawn shops. The flea markets. And Pasar Malam!' She grinned. 'Do you read the *Straits Times* classifieds?'

Nayanika got up and impulsively put her arms around me. 'Now that I've told you my darkest secret, no harm in telling you another: Vani, I'm going to miss you. I really will.'

I hugged her back. At the back of my mind my desire to stay back in Singapore strained at its chains like a frisky dog. I thought of Viren and suddenly felt angry with him.

'I am going to ask Prashanto to speak with your Viren,' said Nayanika. 'He may be able to change his mind.' I shook my head.

I came away from her house feeling better. But I was right. Even though Viren respected Prashanto a lot, he wouldn't budge.

Nayanika, threw a farewell party for us. I had begged Viren to speak to Nita, and he did, to my relief. I wanted my last evening with my circle to be free of any obvious embarrassment. Everybody was sympathetic. They had pooled together to get us some beautiful crystal pieces. Viren laughed and drank with the men. They thumped his back and said that the new century had ushered in a new India. That he was wise to return. That the time was right. It was a beautiful evening. We felt loved by everyone. Yet, my mouth felt full of ashes, and my heart like a lump of lead.

Nita had indeed stayed back. Keeping her head bowed, she'd whispered, 'yes bhaiya', every now and then, when Viren sat her down to explain, as gently as he could. But the minute he went out, she had turned towards me with glittering eyes.

'So bhabhi, no more staying in Singapore, eh?!' She sniggered. 'Why should *you* enjoy the good life? Why? What makes you think you are worth it? You're hardly a beauty. And what did your parents give to my IIT, IIM brother? Hanh? What? Tell me?'

'We are leaving,' I replied. 'Since that makes you so happy.'

'We are leaving!' she mimicked. 'Of course, we are! Did you really think I care for a stupid perfume? Didn't you see what Bhaiya gave me for my birthday?'

Viren had bought her a pair of jade ear studs and a matching locket set in white gold. She brought her jeering face close to mine. I stood stock-still. Her marriage, her second marriage, was almost finalized, barring a few dowry issues, which Viren was going to smoothen out, and he had already convinced the groom. My in-laws would ensure the scandal remained in Singapore. It was a decent match. The groom, an issueless divorcee, came from a broadminded, Western-thinking family, settled in an upmarket Mumbai locality. They had a real estate company and a restaurant. She would have a good life, with holidays abroad. But apparently it was not good enough. A gust of air blew in, sending shivers through my body, squeezing my heart muscles. I was not only being forced to return to India, I was going to go back to something that had the potential to destroy my world. What lingered in the air between us, as I stood before her, stunned and mute, was not the dying aroma of tea dregs in my empty cup. But the scent of something bitter and venomous. Coiled. Ready to strike.

TALL GIRL IN THE RAIN

Amrita stood beneath the diffused orange glow of a rain-drenched street lamp. Standing at five feet and ten inches in her bare feet, Amrita's height was further elevated by her two-inch high formal black shoes, and she stood a good head taller than most of the people who waited alongside her to cross the road. When the green man lit up, they surged across the glistening surface in a single fluid movement. Amrita moved with them, her face billowing above the mass of umbrellas and rain-slicked heads.

It was the elongated hour of a December dusk, another wet day in a month of wind and water. One that held on to moisture like a precious gift, sharpening the scent of earth and foliage. The drizzle that fell on Amrita set her head ablaze with droplets that in turn reflected the colours of polished quartz. She bent forward to receive the rain before it could reach the files, protected inside a plastic bag she clutched to her breast. She hurried, her feet almost skimming across the nearly liquid black stretch of road that reflected back the dark of her eyes. In the wet light, she looked like a delicate preternatural creature almost flying across the black surface. Her mind however was too pre-occupied to notice the quick glances thrown her way. Besides, she did not think she was beautiful. Such an unusual height in an Indian woman is hardly considered an asset. Amrita had heard that so many times, sometimes from kindly and well-meaning relatives, but other times, mostly other times, from the vicious jibes that questioned her very femininity, her worthiness in the eyes of prospective grooms.

Amrita felt plain behind her spectacles and worked hard at being something; anything that could make her height less noticeable. She graduated, and then completed her masters in commerce. She did a course in fashion designing and afterwards, when she got an opportunity to do an MBA at a good institute, she joined that course as well. She worked at a designing house before her marriage, against her parents' wishes. They feared that she would grow too angular as a career woman and subsequently be left on the shelf. But marriage did happen, to Amrita's mother's relief, and the disbelief of the smirking relatives and neighbourhood aunties, when Yash, the son of very distant relatives came to Delhi to visit his parents, and fell in love with the lanky girl he met at a family gathering. He joked that she was the only girl he'd met who could actually look him in the eye without tipping her head backwards. Amrita, diffident and suspicious at first, eventually gave into Yash's curly hair and quizzical eyes. Yash's mother forbade Amrita to wear anything other than the flattest of flat-heeled slippers during the week-long wedding ceremony. Amrita would have continued wearing them had Yash not presented her with a pair of shiny stilettos right after their wedding.

Now Amrita clutched her precious papers, along with something else—a simple faith that at last, after marriage and two children and seven years spent in a country so cold that it seemed to have frozen forever her quietly friendly disposition, that now, when they were in Singapore, as close to India as a developed country could get, she could finally pursue the career that she had put on hold for so long.

Amrita almost ran. The feeder bus that would take her to the MRT station had already arrived. It was getting late, and the place was unfamiliar. The bus was already packed, but Amrita managed to squeeze in. She felt the drip of an umbrella on her already wet shoes. Damp warm bodies pressed and quickly moved away. Mumbled 'sorries' and 'excuse-mes' tumbled over shoulders and backs. It was a relief when the MRT station arrived. A draught of rain-kissed wind stroked her cheek as she alighted. This was familiar terrain. She went down the steps, almost keeping beat with the wind that spiralled down, reached the gates to the platform and inserted her pass.

She found standing space in the compartment which was filled to capacity. Her height gave her a direct view across the heads around her, so she was able to edge forward in time before her stop came. A recorded voice announced City Hall station above the hubbub of people. Amrita crossed over for the connecting train to Kembangan. This time she was lucky. There weren't too many commuters, and she was able to find a seat immediately. Amrita slid off her pumps and rested her aching feet on the cool metal floor of the compartment; the touch soothed her and she twiddled her toes to enhance the feeling, and sank further into her seat. It would take a good twenty minutes before her station arrived.

Amrita and Yash had arrived in Singapore less than six months ago. She had yet to experience that settled in feeling. But they both agreed that Singapore had been far easier to get used to than the towns and cities of Yash's earlier postings. Those other places had been beautiful and intriguing, but also aloof, possibly because Yash's transfer orders had arrived sometimes within weeks of their settling in. So, it had felt like they were on a perpetual journey of discovery as they moved houses in Spain, Germany, France and Switzerland, living for the barest of tenures there, just enough to savour their surroundings, like slow tourists, before moving on to the next country, and the next, and the next, until they reached Holland. The children were born in Holland, giving Amrita scope to grow into something, and discover qualities in herself that she hadn't known before. They made a few friends among the Indian families, but the Dutch community remained out of reach and aloof. Yash had European colleagues who were friendly enough, but they didn't socialize, except for the rare office gathering. Not being able to grasp the language, or reach out to the locals in the casual warm way that came so easily to them, they clung to each other, cradling the babies like delicate saplings whose roots could come apart any minute. Yash shared chores at home. They shopped together for groceries. They went to the houses of their Indian friends where everybody brought their kids. The years trickled past, through the unbearably cold winters and magical but too short summers. Now the boys were in primary school, and they were here, in the Far East.

Yash worked in a large multi-national company. Over the years he had risen in rank and grown senior enough for them to get a company paid transfer to Singapore, a house in a good locality and maid allowance. The last was an unheard-of luxury in their earlier European postings, and Amrita took it to be a good omen. But Singapore was just struggling to recover from a recession, and the omen proved to be less potent than it had first appeared to be. Her initial confident hopes diminished within the first two months of her search. She grew doubtful about her own competence and eligibility.

The people she met during her job searches were polite, but noncommittal. When she returned later for definite answers, she usually failed to meet the one who had interviewed her, and was once again left with a noncommittal response. This happened in places where her credentials were acknowledged before the person on the other side realized that she was not even a Permanent Resident of Singapore. It took Amrita a while to realize that Singaporeans were not comfortable with a direct, in-your-face negative answer. They considered it churlish to spit out an outright 'no'. Their responses were often embedded in circumlocution, leaving her feeling perplexed, and sometimes humiliated. She hung on to a sliver of hope, and then felt let down when her queries remained unanswered. There were occasions, however, when she did come across less traditional, more forthright people who told her, not unkindly, that they did not have a place for her.

Amrita scoured the pages of the *Strait Times* for job vacancies every morning. She diligently trawled the internet for openings. As the days passed, Amrita told herself determinedly that she would take up anything that came even remotely close to her core qualifications. She would not let any opportunity pass her by. Amrita gritted her teeth at this last thought, and an unshed tear gathered underneath her lashes. There was an acute hunger within her, to see herself as something other than Yash's wife and the mother of his boys.

Amrita turned her head to look out of the train as it hurtled like a gigantic metal worm on its metal path, sometimes above the roads and sometimes below. The train was running overhead now and strands of rainwater chased each other down the pane, blurring the squares of cityscape that ran along her line of vision. She closed her eyes as she thought of the morning. The day had begun so pleasantly.

The sun shone in the sky, more like a polished brass plate than a fiery ball. The wet leaves wore a lilt of green where the sun had set his rays down to bask among the foliage after a night of rain. Broken twigs with flame of the forest, queen's flower and frangipani lay scattered on the damp path across the park that Amrita used as a shortcut to Kembangan MRT station. A fragrant vapour rose from the ground. The canal skirting the park gurgled forward, looking for once like a real stream instead of a beatified storm water drain.

There were mostly villas and condominiums skirting the park. It was a locality favoured by well-off locals and white expatriates or *Angmoh,* as the Singaporeans called them, with a few Indian families like Amrita's thrown in between. Dogs and their owners walked at a leisurely pace, savouring the freshly bathed redolence of the park. Amrita had three interviews on her agenda for the day, and that thought along with the prospect of Friday being only a night away filled her with a sense of well-being. She smiled at a few whose faces had become familiar. They smiled back politely before turning away.

The venue for the first of the interviews was at Centre Point, and scheduled for 10.30 a.m. It would take Amrita around forty minutes to reach, but she wanted to keep some buffer time and set off an hour ahead. Once she reached the Orchard Road MRT station, she walked quickly towards the mall where her interview was to take place. The interview didn't last long enough to give her any hope. The lady who interviewed her, seemed kindly. She put her papers in a file with care and told Amrita to call back after a week. That was better than being told that they would get back to her. Amrita thanked her and went out. She walked around the mall to pass the time. It was too early for shoppers, and the sales staff sensing a window shopper, let her browse in peace as they settled in for a new day. By the time Amrita came out, the sky had darkened considerably. Thunder scattered static behind the buildings, and lightening splintered the sky in many places. The next two interviews were to take place after lunch. Amrita had time to kill until then.

Time is a hard task master when there are no tasks at hand, and Amrita felt a cloud shred itself from the sky and enter her, spreading over her heart like a damp cotton quilt. Bracing herself against the changing weather, Amrita walked up and down Orchard Road, eating a chicken wrap that she'd bought at a roadside kiosk. She was lucky. Apart from a few spatters spread far and few, the rain held itself in check. The air around her had a zesty feel about it despite the growing crowd, and the damp quilt slowly began to ease itself out of her heart. Amrita strolled around without looking at her watch, observing the people around her. Most of them wore black suits, sometimes pin-striped in a lighter shade. She still hadn't learnt to distinguish between the Malays and the Chinese among those that wore Western clothes, which in this part of Singapore was more common. Separating the expatriate Indians from the locals had never been a problem for her though. Amrita wondered at this as she watched the men and women come and go.

Finally, Amrita found herself waiting in the lobby of the office where her second interview of the day was scheduled. This company had a chain of clothes stores that sold their own lines of clothing apart from other more established brands. They had plans of expanding beyond Singapore. Amrita was excited about the interview. Her interviewer this time was a man in his forties.

'Mrs Khurana?' He said looking at the door behind her.

Amrita got up to acknowledge her name, but he motioned her to follow him into his cubicle without making eye contact.

'You need a job?'

Amrita paused. He had not even asked her to sit down. 'I am looking for career prospects . . .'

The man grimaced. 'They all say that. Times are bad. Everybody needs a job. If you don't, you have no business to be here.'

'Sir, I did not mean . . .'

'Please sit down, Mrs Khurana. And tell me why we should choose you. Convince me that we need you.'

Amrita breathed. This question was easier to handle, despite her interviewer's brusqueness. Slowly, choosing her words with care, she started to explain how and where she would be able to contribute fruitfully. The man listened to her in silence. He remained silent after she stopped speaking, and continued to contemplate her in silence for so long that Amrita began to feel awkward.

'Well, you seem committed enough. But what about keeping late hours? What about your family? Won't they object? You also have to travel a bit. Are you up to it?'

'That won't be a problem, sir. I have help at home. I can . . .'

'Okay, Mrs Khurana, I will see what I can do. Qualification wise you are fine. There's just one problem; you don't speak either Mandarin or Malay. Knowledge of at least one of the local languages is always a bonus. So, you see, although you seem to be quite good, I can't promise you anything right now. We will get back to you. Okay, la?'

He nodded dismissively at her. Amrita walked towards the door with a metallic taste in her mouth. The next interview was in Ang Mo Kio, at 4.30 p.m. She looked at her watch. It was only 2.45 p.m. This time Amrita walked down Orchard Road, in the opposite direction, towards Takashimaya.

Amrita walked slowly, taking in each floor with a forced sense of leisure. An elegantly attired middle-aged lady selling pearl jewellery from a kiosk at the basement in Takashimaya, smiled at Amrita. Thursday afternoons did not bring in much business, and this slender gazelle of a girl had caught her eye. Amrita smiled back. Encouraged, the lady beckoned, and Amrita, from want of anything better to do, and out of a sense of womanly curiosity, went up to her.

'Where you from, la?' said the pearl lady, smiling.

'India,' said Amrita returning her smile.

'But you so tall, la. So fair. North India?'

'Er . . . Yes. I'm from New Delhi.'

'Oh, New Delhi? Oh yes, yes. North Indians very pretty. Tandoori chicken. My son, he love tandoori chicken, la. So, I learn to make, la! Your family also love tandoori?'

Amrita smiled self-consciously. The lady took a rope of pearls and motioned Amrita to bend her neck. Amrita was startled, but did as she was asked. The lady deftly clasped the pearls around her neck and placed a mirror on the counter.

'I'm sorry, I can't buy,' said Amrita, her cheeks flushing

'No, no, la. No buy. Just you wear now and see,' said the lady smiling broadly now. 'Beautiful neck you have, so slim and long, la! You should tell your husband to get you only beautiful pearls like these ho!'

Amrita touched the pearls at her neck. They felt smooth and cool against her skin. She stood there looking at them for some time, their lustre encircling her throat, lovingly, and tenderly. The lady gently took her hand and slipped a pearl ring on her finger and a bracelet on her wrist. She adjusted the mirror so Amrita could see her throat and hand at the same time. The two women stood there quietly enjoying the mood of the pearls. It was a long magical moment for Amrita, which dissolved as softly as it had arrived when she took off the ring and bracelet. The lady gently unclasped the rope of pearls with soft cool fingers. Amrita felt her touch like a blessing.

'Thank you,' said Amrita huskily, before walking away from the kiosk. The woman smiled and waved. She didn't see the rest of the mall, but walked out as if in a dream, the lady and her pearls lingering on in her mind.

The sky had finally opened up and it poured down sheets of rain, pushing the people against doorways and covered steps. The wind blew the rain in all directions, discharging wetness with precision, but without aim. Amrita stood with the other stranded people. The rain fell on her face like needles. She touched her throat where the pearls had lain a few minutes ago, and found it wet with droplets. She inched back into the mall, and waited.

Once the rain abated, Amrita moved along with the throng towards the long neck of the MRT station, set with rows of shops, called Wisma Atria. The smell of fresh brewed coffee and hot-out-of-the-oven brownies at a newly opened eatery tempted Amrita. She sidestepped into the store to enjoy a brownie.

Amrita sat there for a while contemplating the people around her. She fished out the address from her handbag and looked at it. The address did not throw up any image of the place she was to visit. There was no street name to give her a picture; just the building number followed by an Avenue number something. Maybe she was better off getting into a taxi once she got off at Ang Mo Kio.

When she reached, Amrita was surprised to discover that this last interview of the day was to take place in a shop selling spectacles. The two things that the advertisement had clearly stated were 'very good remuneration package' and 'experience not necessary, training provided'. She had assumed it would be an office. The shopping complex where it was located seemed shabby compared to the ones she had been to earlier in the day. Amrita hesitated before the glass door. An old man squatting in the corridor drinking Teh Tarik smiled at her toothlessly and motioned her to go in. He nodded and pointed towards the door. The rest of the people, in their shops and kiosks, ignored her. Styrofoam cups and soda cans lay in a heap near a bin. A stray cat minced its way through the trash. Amrita inhaled the mingled odours of Pandan leaves and Durian and quickly exhaled as she went in.

An earnest looking, bespectacled man looked at her owlishly. 'Yes?'

'You advertised for sales manager?'

'Ah. Yes, yes, yes. Please take a seat. I explain scheme to you, la.'

Amrita sat down; her fingers ready with her papers. But the man seemed least interested. He sucked in his breath and launched into a memorized selling spiel about a scheme that Amrita could barely comprehend. The man talked nonstop for ten minutes, at the end of which he sucked in his breath again.

'Very good policy, la. You make good money, la. Just deposit two hundred dollar, la, get returns, 20 per cent. One-time only deposit. You sell policy to others, get big–big returns . . .'

Amrita stared at the man until he became a blur. Only his lenses gleamed back at her like a pair of cat's eyes in the dark. Amrita rose from her seat like a somnambulist and left without saying a word. Behind her the man sucked in his breath like a secret that had spilled and now must be quickly gathered in. The door closed behind Amrita with sibilant urgency.

The rain was a dull drizzle by the time she reached the road outside the shopping centre. Clutching her files close, Amrita found herself walking in the rain towards the bus stop.

'Next stop Kembangan,' announced the recorded voice.

Amrita raised her head as the disembodied voice cut into her reverie. Her fingers were numb from clutching her files. She let herself out as the doors slid open. Once outside, she hurried forward, almost running towards the park that would take her home to Yash. The canal slunk along beside her, occasionally winking back at the lights from the houses on the other side. Her feet squelched loudly on the wet path of the empty park. She moved swiftly under the dark moisture-laden trees, a feeling of dread giving speed to her feet. She slowed her pace only when she saw the street lamp's welcoming light outside their gate.

She found Yash waiting for her when she entered. The boys were in their bedroom trying to have a pillow fight as quietly as possible. The maid was with them in their room. She would not come out until called to serve their dinner. He watched her as she took off her damp shoes. She shook her hair free of droplets before slipping into a pair of rubber flip-flops. Her neck looked fragile, like a delicate stalk holding up a tulip. He almost smiled at the thought; he had never thought of tulips with regard to Amrita in Holland. He must not forget to tell her that she had blossomed into one only after coming to Singapore. She saw him looking at her and smiled, but her smile was more bud and less bloom.

He did not ask her how she had fared in the interviews. He silently handed her a glass of Hennessy. They sat on the couch together, holding their glasses, not speaking, not touching; not even looking at each other. He waited for her to speak. He knew her words would not come until later, much later.

Lately Yash had been noticing small changes in Amrita—how her pale fingers fluttered ever so slightly when she moved, and how she had begun to wrap gauzy lengths of silence about her. Her shoulders had begun to stoop ever so little between the words. Her eyes looked like deep wells that could not reflect back light. And when at last her words came out in twos and threes, they were often muffled.

He waited nonetheless, and she sought his patiently waiting presence, the same way she sought the sweet-smelling spaces between the silver slants of falling rain. They sat with their glasses warming in their hands, listening to the rain as it drummed and thrummed its songs on the mosquito-mesh covered windows. In the dim gold light of their parlour, only the rain's voice spoke.

ACKNOWLEDGEMENTS

Journals and magazines that publish short fiction and other creative works are writers' friends and allies. Editors are the good fairies who help writers keep the faith, shining a light down that solitary and stony path. I am no exception. There are so many to thank. I'll begin with my editors Manasi Subramaniam, Aparna Kumar and others at Penguin Random House India, who took this journey with me, giving me necessary shots of enthusiasm, editorial advice and encouragement. Also, Aditya Mani Jha, who first commissioned *Impetuous Women*.

My thanks to Indira Chandrasekhar who first published two of the stories in this collection in Out of Print, India. My thanks too, to the following editors: Novelist Soniah Kamal who picked my story for Sugar Mule, USA; Miriam Kotzin, editor of Per Contra, USA; Monideepa Sahu, co-editor, and Zafar Anjum, editor and publisher of The Best Asian Short Stories 2017, Kitaab, Singapore; Vaishali Khandekar, editor of Reading Hour, India; Beate Sigriddaughter, editor of Writing in a Woman's Voice, USA, and the editors of India Currents along with Prajwal Parajuly and Amulya Malladi, judges of the Katha Short Story Prize 2016.

I also want to thank my family—my son and husband, but most of all my daughter, for being there and creating the spaces necessary for a writer, especially one who is often daft and cranky.

The following stories were previously published:

'Taste'—Out of Print, India

'Threshold'—Sugar Mule, USA

'The Amma Who Took French Leave'—Per Contra, USA

'Miz Tiga Does Not Play Holi'—The Paumanok Review, USA

'Patchwork'—The Best Asian Short Stories 2017, Kitaab Publications, Singapore

'Marital Bliss'—Wired Ruby, USA

'Just Desserts'—Broadsheet, UK, as 'Sweet Surprise'

'Missing the Movie'—Danse Macabre, USA

'It Comes from Uranus'—India Currents, USA

'Word among Poets'—Out of Print, India

'Feral'—The Reading Hour, India

'Tall Girl in the Rain'—Writing in a Woman's Voice, USA